UNTIL THE SUN RISES

MICHELE SIMS

This is a work of fiction. Names, characters, places and incidents are products of the author's imagination or are used fictitiously and should not be construed as real. Any resemblance to actual events, locales, organizations or persons, living or dead, is entirely coincidental.

Until The Sun Rises by Michele Sims

ISBN: Ebook- 978-1-7347567-8-4
Print- 978-1-7347567-9-1

Green Books Publishing, LLC

Book cover design and Interior formatting by 100 Covers.

Contents

Dedication

I dedicate this book to all those who believe

there is no greater power than love and

to those who know true love never dies.

How it all began...

Want to know the origin of Carly and Mace's unforgettable love story? I invite you to read FOREVER CARLY, *the first book in my* **Second Chance Series**, *where passion, heartbreak, and hope collide during a Charleston Christmas.* UNTIL THE SUN RISES *can absolutely be read as a standalone—but for readers who crave rich backstory and emotional depth, Carly and Mace's journey is the satisfyingly delicious beginning that makes everything that follows even more meaningful. Below is the blurb for* FOREVER CARLY—*your invitation to fall in love from the very first page.*

What if everything you worked for—your career, your marriage, your dreams—was torn away by betrayal?

What if coming home for Christmas didn't feel like a celebration, but a last chance to piece together the shattered parts of your life?

That's where we find Dr. Carly Rivers.

Battered by a cruel divorce. Worn down by a brutal legal battle. Heartbroken by the thought of losing the one place that ever felt like home.

And just when she thinks she's lost everything, fate steps in... wearing the familiar face of her first love.

FOREVER CARLY *is a story about heartbreak and hope. About risking it all when you have every reason to run. It's about choosing love—choosing yourself—even when the past tries to drag you under.*

It's messy, it's beautiful, and it's exactly the kind of story that reminds us: the heart may break, but it never forgets how to love again.

Introduction

Mason Moore was no ordinary man. He was a modern-day prince, anointed at birth with the keys to his family's fortune. Famous, powerful, and desired by many, he was one of Charleston's most eligible bachelors. Yet somehow, beyond my wildest imagination, he loved me. His heart, his loyalty—everything that made him the man I couldn't live without—belonged to me.

We were given a second chance, and without hesitation, I flew away with him to the sun-soaked island of Barbados. No elaborate reception, no family or friends, just us, bound together in love. I never cared about the fantasy of saying yes to a dress, so I didn't mourn the loss of a fairy tale wedding. Instead, we created something far more meaningful.

On that perfect February fourteenth, we stood barefoot on the beach, wrapped in the embrace of a glowing sunset. The sky painted itself in fiery streaks of pink, orange, and gold, as if the universe itself was celebrating our union. The gentle breeze whispered through the trees, nature's quiet blessing, as we became husband and wife. It was just the minister, his wife, Mason and me, nothing to distract me from the overwhelming love in his eyes and the warmth of his hand holding mine.

As we walked back to our secluded villa, he made a promise that filled me with excitement and hope: "When we return to Charleston, we'll share our happiness with everyone we love. I'm going to throw the grandest party this city has ever seen." His words were full of joy, but they were also a vow to live a life of adventure, romance, and an unbreakable bond.

But as we reveled in our bliss, oblivious to the world, we unknowingly ignited something dangerous. Jealousy. The shadows of others who resented what we had, what they couldn't find for themselves. They watched us, their bitterness creeping in like a storm on the horizon. We were so naive, so lost in the magic of what we had, that we didn't see the darkness closing in until it was too late.

Our love was powerful, but could it survive the forces determined to tear us apart? Would we pay a high price for it as our lives spiraled into a dark abyss before we could find our way back to the light?

Forever,

Carly

Chapter One

MASON Moore opened his eyes slowly, taking in the familiar expanse of his executive office in downtown Charleston. The leather chair creaked under him as he stretched, a reminder of the life he'd built—no, *fought* to achieve. The opulence of the room echoed his success. He couldn't believe his fortune. Life was better than any dream he could've conjured: a thriving business, powerful contacts, and best of all, a beautiful wife who brought fire into every part of his life. Or so it seemed.

His thoughts lingered on Carly, his wife, expecting their child, humming softly in the adjoining bathroom. Her presence was like a warm embrace, comforting yet electrifying. She had surprised him that morning with a visit before he could start his long day of meetings. Only moments after her arrival, she had been sitting on his lap, legs draped over his, reminding him of the promise he'd almost forgotten.

"Mace, you know we have rules," she'd said with a mischievous grin, tilting his chin up toward her. "You never leave the house without saying goodbye. You promised."

"I'm sorry," he had murmured, entirely too distracted by her lips to give a proper apology. He let his hands wander over her thighs, reveling in the feel of her warmth. "But I'm willing to make it up to you."

He had barely finished the sentence before Carly leaned in, capturing his lips in a kiss that was nothing short of devouring. Her fingers tangled in his hair as she deepened the kiss, making him feel as though

he was on fire. The woman was relentless in her demands, and he was all too happy to surrender.

"This is what you'll miss," she had teased, nibbling his lower lip and sending jolts of pleasure through him. "If you leave the house without saying goodbye again."

"I won't do it again," he had whispered, his voice hoarse as her teeth grazed his neck. The playful sting of her bite made him groan. "You win, Carly. Always."

But before the morning's play could escalate into something more, Carly had slipped away to freshen up in his office bathroom, leaving Mace sitting there, shirt half-unbuttoned, mind swirling with thoughts of her. He smiled, thinking of the way she had taken control, always knowing how to push his buttons.

His grin didn't even fade when a commotion outside his door broke his reverie.

"You can't just barge in!" His assistant, Andrew, sounded flustered.

"I'm not leaving until I see him," a sharp female voice retorted, followed by the unmistakable sound of the office door slamming open.

Mace barely had time to stand and fasten his belt buckle before a woman he vaguely recognized stormed into his office. She was impeccably dressed in a tailored black suit, her heels clicking sharply against the floor as she advanced, fire in her eyes.

"Who the hell are you?" Mace demanded, anger simmering.

The woman squared her shoulders, planted her hands on her hips, and defiantly jutted out her chin. "I'm Nala Clarke. Maybe you don't remember me, but our mothers know each other. I've spoken to you at multiple events."

Mace shook his head, barely listening as his mind raced to catch up. *Who is this woman, and why is she here*?

Before he could respond, Carly emerged from the bathroom, her hair in a messy bun and her yoga clothes hugging her curves. She looked at Nala, then at Mace, and a slow, cautious smirk crept across her face. "What's going on here?"

Nala, apparently unperturbed by Carly's arrival, continued, "Your fancy wedding reception ruined my life."

Carly stepped closer to Mace, her presence instantly grounding him. "Excuse me?"

Mace was about to intervene, but Carly gave him a look that said, "Let me handle this".

Nala's gaze flicked between them, her confidence seeming to waver for a moment. "My fiancé—ex-fiancé—called off our wedding one week before the ceremony. We were supposed to get married the same day as your lavish, last-minute reception, and after it was announced as the event of the season, my guests canceled on me. The venue canceled saying I was in breach of contract. My floral designer canceled. The caterer canceled.

"And eventually… so did he." Her voice trembled as she spoke, fists clenched at her sides. "He felt what was happening was a bad omen."

Maybe you should have finished paying your vendors what you owed them. I did. Mace held his peace, not wanting to add fuel to the fire by sharing that the vendors had told him she hadn't finished paying her debts.

Carly didn't break eye contact with Nala. "And how is that our fault?"

Nala's eyes flashed with anger. "You people," she spat, her voice dripping with venom, "you think you can just throw money around and make everything go your way. You stole my day."

Mace instinctively placed his arm around Carly's waist, pulling her closer. "We didn't steal anything," he said firmly, though he felt Carly gently squeeze his hand, a signal to let her take the lead.

Before either could say more, the office door opened again, and Attorney Ariel Dennison, one of Carly's best friends, entered the room, her face a mixture of confusion and concern. "Hey, Carly," Ariel said, casting a wary glance at Nala. "Am I interrupting something?"

"Not at all," Carly replied, her voice light yet tinged with an underlying sharpness. "There seems to be a misunderstanding of a lot of things."

Ariel raised an eyebrow, obviously sensing the conflict. "Should I stick around?"

"Please," Carly said, smiling. "This won't take long."

Mace looked between the three women, feeling the air in the room shift. Nala, for all her bravado, was clearly outnumbered, but Carly was handling it with grace and strength that made him love her even more.

Nala blinked rapidly, her anger faltering. "I just… I lost everything," she whispered.

Carly stepped forward, her voice soft but firm. "I'm sorry for what you've been through, but we didn't cause this. And as for your fiancé, if he bailed over something like this, maybe you dodged a bullet. You'll have to find peace some other way instead of blaming us."

Nala stood there for a moment, chest rising and falling as she tried to steady her breath. Someone has to pay," she said, but the threat lacked its earlier venom.

Mace, who had been silent through the exchange, finally spoke. "We're sorry your day didn't go as planned, Nala, but we can't be held responsible for decisions other people made. Now, if there's nothing else, I think it's time for you to leave."

Nala's eyes glistened with unshed tears, but her expression hardened. "You think this is over? It's not. I'm suing my ex for everything he put me through. And I'm coming after you too, Mace Moore. You and your wife will pay for what you did to me." Her voice quivered with anger, but there was an eerie calm behind her words, a quiet promise of more to come.

Before Mace could react, Andrew, Mace's assistant, reappeared in the doorway with security. "Miss Clarke," he gestured to the uniformed officer standing beside him, "it's time for you to leave."

Nala shot one last menacing look at Mace and Carly before turning on her heel. "This isn't over," she muttered as the officer led her out.

Ariel crossed her arms, letting out a low whistle. "What the hell just happened?"

Mace sighed heavily, rubbing his temples as the weight of her words settled like lead in his gut. "I don't even know anymore."

"No good deed," Carly muttered as Mace pulled her close, "goes unpunished."

Mace nodded, though the tension in his body didn't ease. As much as he wanted to believe it was just an empty threat, something in Nala's parting words had left a chill in the air. He let out a long breath and kissed Carly's temple. "You handled that beautifully."

Carly turned in his arms, resting her head on his chest. "I don't know about that. But I'm glad it's over."

Ariel cleared her throat. "Um, are we still going to yoga class?" she reminded Carly with a grin.

Carly chuckled, turning to her friend. "I could use a workout now."

Mace squeezed Carly tighter for a moment before releasing her. "Enjoy your class. I'll see you at home this evening. I can't wait for round two." He kissed her lips before she left with Ariel.

"Mr. Moore, your attorney is on the line," Andrew interrupted from the doorway.

Mace glanced at the phone, his face hardening. "What now?"

Chapter Two

CARLY pulled into the concrete driveway on the side of her aunt's home on Henrietta Street and waved. Her aunt was sitting in one of her white rocking chairs on the wraparound porch. Carly always liked it when the weather was warm, with a slight breeze that allowed them the chance to enjoy each other's company outside while sipping lemonade or tea.

"Good morning, Aunt Nora." Carly got out of the car and closed the door.

She climbed the brick stairs as she had done so many times before, touching the wood railing matching the trim around the front of the home. Her aunt had always painted the ceiling of the porch blue, a Charleston tradition to keep away the bad spirits.

Aunt Nora, a woman who had grown more beautiful with age, was dressed in a casual floral cotton dress. She rose from her seat and greeted Carly with a warm embrace. She smiled with her whole face, a familiar expression with the twinkle in her eyes. Carly never took that smile for granted, as it reminded her that she and her brother, John, were much loved.

"You're right on time dear." Aunt Nora held on to the arms of her chair, returning to her seat. "I just finished fixing this lemonade. Do you want some?" She placed her hand on the pitcher's glass handle and grabbed one of the matching tall glasses with her other hand.

"Yes, thank you." Carly took a seat next to her aunt around the table. She smoothed back her hair and stretched before rotating her shoulders. "I needed that yoga class this morning." She took the glass of lemonade from her aunt's outstretched hand, and after her first sip, she closed her eyes and exhaled. "Oh, this is so good."

"Glad you like it." Her aunt smiled. "I guess you're still recovering from that big party Mace had."

Carly nodded, her face covered with a bright smile. "Before I forget, Ariel is in town. I told her to meet me here after she returned a few phone calls." She buried her lips between her teeth and looked away.

"Great. It'll be good to catch up with Ariel. I didn't have much time to talk with her at the reception." Aunt Nora refreshed their glasses with more lemonade. "I'm still hearing about your reception, weeks later. Everyone commented on how beautiful you looked."

"I'm still hearing about it too." Carly sat back and rocked as she took sips of her cool drink. She placed the glass to her forehead and cheek, allowing the condensation forming on the glass to drip down the side of her face, distracting her from her thoughts.

"I was surprised how well you recreated your cousin's wedding reception, the one you attended as a little girl, with so little time to plan it." Aunt Nora rubbed her chin. "I don't know how you did it."

"What reception?" Carly placed her glass on the table and drew her brows together, staring at her aunt.

"Girl!" Aunt Nora's hands made a slapping sound as they landed in her lap. "If you didn't talk about that wedding a thousand times with your mother and me, you didn't mention it at all." She sat back and rocked in the chair. "We took you to your cousin's wedding when you were about eight years old, one of the fanciest weddings our family had ever had. It was at the Mills House—you know, downtown on Meeting Street."

"Yes, I know where it is." Carly turned and settled comfortably in her seat.

"We entered the ballroom and had to pull you in the room." She let out a small laugh. "You were so mesmerized by all the grand decorations that you stopped in your tracks and refused to move until you'd had a chance to look around. I guess it was a sight to see because, as an adult, I was impressed too. I felt rich and important to just be in the room and I wasn't expected to serve anyone." Aunt Nora's smile faded a bit as she paused, inhaling a deep breath. "Well, it was like we were invited to an event straight out of a fairy tale." She looked up at Carly. The glint had returned to her eyes.

"I remember vaguely, as a little girl, going to a big wedding." Carly tilted her head.

"There were ice sculptures of doves and wedding bells all around the room. I had never seen anything like that before. They sparkled like diamonds when the lights hit them," Aunt Nora reminisced.

Carly sat up, allowing the beautiful, shared memories to envelop them as Aunt Nora continued.

"A feast of different foods like it was prepared for royalty covered the tables adorned with large floral centerpieces and yards of satin, tulle, and lace. I recall that there were soft pink and white flowers surrounded by lush greenery in the corners of the room. The waiters were all dressed in tuxedos with tails and…" Carly abruptly stood, causing Aunt Nora to pause. "What's wrong, sweetheart?"

Carly placed a hand over her heart, silence substituting for a verbal response.

"Tell me what's happening, Carly?" She placed a hand on Carly's arm as tears fell from Carly's eyes. "Have a seat and tell me what's going on."

Carly heeded Aunt Nora's advice and slowly returned to her seat. "He's in trouble because of me." She leaned her elbow on the table and placed her fist to her mouth.

"Who's in trouble?" Aunt Nora's eyes widened. She lowered Carly's fist from her mouth and nodded, urging her to speak.

"It's Mace." Carly rubbed her forehead. "When we were in Barbados on our honeymoon, enjoying our night together. I was a little worn out—in a good way." She chuckled. "Until just now, I thought

I had dreamt that I told Mace about that reception, but it must have really happened. We were naked on a private stretch of beach and—"

"Dear, you can skip that part," Aunt Nora advised, rubbing the back of her neck. "Tell me what you told him about the reception."

"He was resting on his elbow beside me, and he asked me that night after we eloped to describe what a fairy tale wedding would look like to me." She looked away, focusing on the memory of the first night she'd shared with Mace as his wife. "That's when I must have told him about our cousin's wedding. With all the emotions swirling around my head after agreeing to elope, the surprise reception Mace had planned when we returned to Charleston, and missing Mom, I didn't realize that he had recreated the wedding reception of my dreams."

"So, Mace planned the whole thing by himself?" Aunt Nora's mouth slackened.

"He had the help of an event planner, but he told her what he wanted." Carly shook her head. "He promised me the reception of my dreams." Her eyes glistened.

"And he delivered," Aunt Nora replied with a slap on her knee. "So, why is he in trouble?"

"If I wasn't in Mace's office this morning to see it, I wouldn't believe it myself." Carly ran her hand through her hair. "He was threatened with being sued." She allowed herself a faint smile. Drawing her knees to her chest, she sat back in the chair. "A young lady named Nala Clarke came to his office this morning and told Mace that he ruined her life by having our reception on what was supposed to be her wedding day. She blames him that her wedding was called off."

"Now that's a stretch." Aunt Nora rolled her eyes, extending her arms in the air. "Nala needs to stop it."

"You know her?" Carly pursed her lips.

"I know her mother, Alexandra Clarke. She and I served on several charitable boards together. Her father, Nicholas, and my husband, Hank, were friends. Sadly, they've both gone to glory and Alexandra is suffering from dementia. She's in a long-term care home. The past few years haven't been good for her. Their son, Simeon, is running the family's business."

"Sorry to hear about the Clarkes. That does help to explain Nala's poor choices."

Aunt Nora cocked her head. "You're telling me that she's blaming Mace, who did everything to please you, his wife, for her inability to hold on to her man? I'll be darned."

"Well, it's more than that. She mentioned that she was also trying to retrieve the money she'd lost and recover from the embarrassment her failed engagement caused."

"What are you all going to do about it?" Aunt Nora leaned forward.

Carly shrugged. "Mace didn't seem fazed by her accusations."

"I wouldn't underestimate that little tart. Her beauty has always been the light that draws people to her, but from the time she was a little girl, I always sensed a darkness, not on the surface, but somewhere inside her. There's something not right about her. Mark my words." Aunt Nora shuddered as if a cold wind had just blown past her.

"I agree." Carly tugged at her earlobe. "She's no Miss Innocent."

A blue Mercedes rolled into the driveway. Ariel cut the motor and grabbed her handbag before opening the door.

"Hi, Auntie Nora." Ariel flashed a bright toothy smile. "Carly, I'm glad the two of you are outside on this beautiful day. I have some news to share." She made her way toward the porch.

"Good, come sit a while." Aunt Nora rose to greet her. "Let me get some more refreshments for all of us."

"Do you have any of those delicious tea biscuits?" Ariel licked her lips.

"I sure do." Aunt Nora grabbed the pitcher and turned to enter the house. "Coming right up."

Ariel directed her response to Carly. "We might need them. Something a little sweet to make the reality easier to swallow."

Gazing at the ceiling, Carly remarked, "What else could happen?"

Before Ariel could answer, Aunt Nora returned, balancing a tray of ginger tea and her famous biscuits. "I'm glad you girls are back on speaking terms."

Carly noticed the subtle way her aunt's eyes lingered on her, a silent concern Carly had grown used to ever since she'd announced her pregnancy, still in its early stages. Aunt Nora set the tray down gently, her hands steady but her gaze filled with protective love.

"Help yourselves," she said, though Carly sensed she wanted to say more.

Ariel poured the tea, her movements deliberate, but Carly felt the strain beneath Ariel's calm exterior.

"Carly knew Yara and I would always have her back. We couldn't stay mad at her for long," Ariel said, giving Carly a sideways glance, the sting of her elopement still fresh between them. "But we were more disappointed than anything. We couldn't imagine you getting married without us. We weren't there for your special day."

Ariel took a bite of her biscuit, honey dripping from the corner of her mouth as she closed her eyes in pleasure. "Auntie Nora, these are as good as ever." Ariel dabbed her mouth and cocked her head toward Aunt Nora. "I was surprised at how well you took the news about the elopement."

"Of course, I wanted to be there," Aunt Nora replied, her voice soft but firm. "But when I thought about it, I realized how much it saved my girl to elope. Paying for an expensive wedding and reception? That could have been a disaster." She glanced at Carly, her eyes full of determination. "If I'd had to take out a mortgage to help her, I would've, but I'm glad I didn't have to."

Carly placed a hand over her aunt's, her heart swelling with both gratitude and guilt. "I couldn't have asked you to do that. Before you reminded me of my reaction to our cousin's wedding, I thought that I never wanted anything that grand for myself." She smiled, though the edges of it were tinged with unease. "Mace insisted on eloping. There was no talking him into a small wedding. Money wasn't the problem, it was time. He wanted to marry me right away." She hesitated, instinctively resting a hand on her stomach. “We both love Barbados, so he flew us there on his jet.”

“And it all worked out,” Aunt Nora said, her expression softening. “We were there when you two made your debut as husband and wife back in Charleston.”

Ariel shifted in her seat, her tone sharpening. “Worked out, sure, but not without fallout.” She met Carly’s eyes. “Did you tell Auntie Nora about Nala?”

Carly nodded, though the mention of Nala brought a dull ache to her stomach. She absently rubbed her belly, more concerned about the stress than the woman herself. “She knows.”

Ariel pulled out her phone, her fingers tapping rapidly. “Okay, so here’s what I found out. Since your beautiful wedding reception, everyone in Charleston’s been talking about you. And not just talking, trying to get close to you. And then, there’s Nala.” She paused, showing Carly the screen. “Since you became ‘Mrs. Mason Moore,’ it’s like people can’t get enough of you. Social media’s blowing up with influencers trying to snap pictures of you. Some are even calling you and Mace ‘MacCarly.’”

Carly rolled her eyes, her fingers nervously brushing the crystal cover of Ariel’s phone. “We are not a power couple.”

Ariel raised an eyebrow and turned the screen toward her. “Oh, but you are. And Nala? She’s playing a longer game. I looked at the posts on her socials. She recently signed up for your seminar at the university. And that’s not all. Since your reception, people have been scrambling to join anything you’re involved in. They want to be seen with you. Nala’s name on your class roster? That’s no coincidence.”

Carly frowned, a ripple of anxiety moving through her. She wasn’t one to dismiss concerns, but she didn’t see Nala as a real threat—at least, not yet. “It’s just… weird. I get it, she’s suing Mace, but she’s also free to take any class she wants, isn’t she?”

“Technically, yes,” Ariel said, her eyes narrowing. “I talked to the university after the incident this morning. There are only three reasons they can bar someone from enrolling in a class: misconduct, threatening behavior, or a crime. Nala’s clean on all fronts.”

Carly rubbed her stomach absentmindedly, a deep breath slipping out as the tension around them grew heavier. "I just don't understand why she's so interested in me. Or Mace."

"She's got over a hundred thousand followers. Maybe she's looking for content," Ariel warned, leaning back in her chair. "My advice? Don't engage. She could be waiting for you to make a mistake."

"I won't let her get to me," Carly said, though a glimmer of doubt lingered in her mind. Her phone pinged, and Carly relaxed when she saw the message from Mace. "That was Mace. He'll be home in time for dinner."

"Did he meet with Evan today?" Aunt Nora asked, her brows furrowed with concern. "His brother's a sharp lawyer. He'll know how to handle this."

"They were supposed to meet today," Carly replied, finishing her biscuit, though it tasted hollow now. The unease settled deeper. "I'm sure Evan's on top of it."

Aunt Nora placed a hand on Carly's arm, her voice softening. "You need to stay off social media, honey. Especially with the baby on the way. Stress isn't good for either of you."

Carly sighed, nodding. "I know, Aunt Nora, but I can't. Not if I want tenure at the university in the history department. I need to stay connected, keep my research visible." She looked at Ariel, the weight of expectation heavy on her shoulders. "That's how the Renovate Charleston project came together. I used social media to bring in community support for it."

Ariel gave her a pointed look. "I went to the site online and fifteen people signed up for the Renovate Charleston the same hour as Nala. Another coincidence? I think not."

Carly leaned back in her chair, trying to push the worry away, though it clung to her like a shadow. "Maybe. But I just can't see her as a real threat."

Ariel shrugged, grabbing her bag. "Just be careful. Fame draws people to you, and not always the ones you want around."

"I will," Carly promised, though deep down, she wasn't sure how much longer she could ignore the growing presence of Nala in her life. "I planned to give her space enough to hang herself. I don't know much about her, but first impressions… she's not my cup of tea." She and Ariel shared a laugh.

"Do you still want to go shopping downtown?" Ariel asked. "I still have time before I need to pack for my trip home tomorrow."

"Yes, I have some pieces I want to purchase from the lingerie shop on King Street that hosted my bridal shower. Let's also stop by Hampden's. They have a professional stylist who really gets me. She called to say that some of the fashions I ordered are in." Carly smiled.

"Do you have time to swing by Tiny Tassel?" Ariel rose from her seat.

"Sure thing. We can swing by the condo, shower and change before we go. Looks like we're going to be shopping all day. Auntie, do you want to come with us?"

"No." She stood and cleared the table. "You two have fun. I'll catch up with you later."

"I'm glad you've decided to accept Mace's offer to expand your wardrobe." Ariel grabbed her bag off the table and crossed her arms. "You have some great two-piece business suits for the classroom, but now that you're the wife of a rich man, it's time to try new things."

"I didn't choose to be a history professor because I wanted a glamorous career." Carly pursed her lips. "Are you saying that I don't have the right clothes for Mace's social circle?" Carly placed her hands on her hips. "Do I have a standard to uphold now that I'm the wife of a man whose first wife was a supermodel?"

"If you have to ask, girlfriend…" Ariel gave her a knowing look.

"I get it." Carly nodded. "Let's take my car."

Chapter Three

"I'M still trying to figure out what just happened." Mace walked back and forth, running his hands through his hair. "One minute, I'm enjoying a great start to the day with my wife and the next"—he looked at his brother Evan, seated behind his desk in his law office—"some woman barges into my office to tell me that I ruined her life." His voice hardened as he took off his jacket containing his phone and threw it on the couch. It hit with a thud. "Sorry, bruh." He resumed pacing.

"Calm down," Evan assured him, holding his palms in the air. "Like I told you on the phone and I repeat now, she doesn't have a case."

"She has a lawyer, and if that's so, why would any lawyer accept the case?" He stopped and looked back over his shoulder.

"People have different motivations for their actions." Evan shrugged. "Maybe someone took the case as a favor to her or her family, and there's always the hope that you'll settle to make this go away."

"No way." He narrowed his eyes with a steely resolve. "I'm not settling."

"I agree with that." Evan loosened his tie. "This is a good case to play hard ball. We don't want anyone else to look at you as a case for civil suit lottery."

"I'm angry that Carly has to get caught up in this mess." Mace took the seat that Evan had offered earlier. "I could see by the look in her eyes, the one she had when she comforted a wounded puppy when we were kids, that she felt for the girl. She was buying some of the story."

Evan nodded. "Carly has a good heart, but she's also smart. No one plays her for a fool."

"I agree." Mace stroked his chin.

"Maybe you should suggest that she go on vacation with my family and Mom. Kate and the kids would love to have her hang out with them." He placed his hands on the desk. "They're in California for a week of spring break."

"It won't work." Mace looked at the ceiling. "We haven't been back from our honeymoon for a month yet and I'm supposed to suggest she go away without me?"

"I see your point. Why don't you go too?"

He stared at Evan. "And appear that I'm cutting and running?" He frowned. "No way. This is going to somehow appear in social media and make me look like I have something to hide."

"It's good that you bring up the point of social media." Evan got up and went to the mini fridge on the other side of his desk. "Water?"

"You got anything stronger?" Mace watched as Evan went to the bar. "It's after five o'clock and I could use a cocktail. It's been a long day." He rolled up his sleeves.

"You've got to watch what you say." Evan poured the drinks. "You don't want this case tried in the court of public opinion." He handed the glass to Mace. "It wouldn't look good if you, the big bad businessman, appeared to be using his money, power, and position to bully a young woman who just wanted to enjoy what she thought would be the best day of her life. Some may think you robbed her of that chance."

"What?" Mace yelled. "Her failed wedding was her problem."

"We both know that, but sympathy doesn't have to be logical." Evan took a long sip of his drink. "If they persist in taking this to court, it's my job to make our argument make sense. I won't have a problem doing that."

Mace smiled for the first time. "Have you started getting information on her? I mean, doing a background search?"

"Yes, we have, but don't think they haven't been doing research on our family in Charleston as well."

"What kind of research?" Mace cocked a brow.

"For one, how we got our money." Evan placed his glass on the table between the chairs separating them. "You know some of the property that we inherited from Pop, our grandfather, was taken in what could be described as a land grab."

"Pop understood opportunity," Mace responded before finishing his drink. Crossing his arms, he maintained a defensive posture. "No one is going to smear the name of Mason Jefferson, our grandfather, as long as I'm alive." He frowned. "He was a good businessman. He never stole from anyone. I took my portion of the inheritance from him, and I worked my ass off for over a decade to grow it from a local business to an organization that has a place on the international stage."

"I agree, but anyone can spin a story how they wish. Again, if they wanted to show that the Moores have a history of using their position to take or rob others of what rightfully belonged to them, this could be an angle. Don't get me wrong," Evan advised, sitting back in his chair, "I think you're bulletproof, but her legal team is going after the deepest pockets they can find. They didn't file a suit against you personally, and none of the contracts that were signed with the vendors for the reception were signed by you. The contractual agreement was with one of the private subsidiaries of Moore Investment Group. Your assistants made the arrangements and signed the contracts on your behalf. There's no proof that you were even aware of the details, so no one can provide evidence that you had an intent to destroy Nala's special day as she's insinuating."

"More like imagining." Mace snickered.

"Your business reputation as one who gets what he wants, the anti-choirboy, could also be used against you." Evan cupped his index finger, pressing it against the rim of his lip. "You've not been known for displaying your kinder, gentler side. Also, the mess with your ex-wife, Jamillah, won't help. She was very vocal that it took years to get what she thought she deserved in the divorce settlement."

"I'm not worried about Jamillah." Mace sighed. "I increased her portion of the profits from the sale of the business we once owned together." He massaged the muscles in the back of his neck, which were tightening from talking about Jamillah. "She's moved on with her life. We're finally in each other's rearview mirror."

"That's good to know." Evan tented his fingers.

"Just say it," Mace urged. "I can tell you're deciding how to say what you're thinking."

"Okay." Evan rubbed the back of his neck with his hand. "You and Carly have a second chance at love. It's your reality, and it could play well in the press. You've found your way back to each other after a decade apart, and many people know that. They've been rooting for the two of you. Let them see the two of you together, smiling and embracing like newlyweds do."

Mace pondered as his lips tightened. "Forgive me, but I'm not putting on a show for anyone. I love my wife, and I'm grateful to have her back in my life."

"That's the point, Mason. Let that side of you, the softer side that genuinely comes out when you're around Carly, show for everyone to see. It's real." Evan smiled. "I've never seen you smile, dance, or hug anyone as much as you loved on your wifey at your reception. Even a blind man could see how much you love and adore her."

He remained silent as his heart swelled with emotion. Mace swallowed the hard lump in his throat. He wasn't comfortable that his true feelings had been on display to be used by others. After all, hadn't he spent a decade hiding his feelings, being unreadable and winning at business? Hell yeah. But with Carly, he didn't care who knew how much he loved her.

"I love my wife, and I would do it again to see that smile on her face as we danced together for the first time as man and wife. She's my priority, but I'm not going to treat my marriage like it's something for public consumption. You know how folks hailing and praising you today can be the same folks nailing you tomorrow."

"I get it," Evan agreed.

Mace looked at his watch. "Damn, I told Carly I'd be home in time for dinner." He grabbed his jacket before rushing out of the office. "Thanks for the advice."

***

Carly sank into the plush leather couch, her fingers absently tracing the soft edges of a throw pillow. The warm glow from the city lights outside played across the sleek silver accents of their downtown Charleston condo. The space felt empty without Mace, its cool modern design somehow amplifying her loneliness tonight. She sighed and rubbed her belly, her fingers brushing over the curve of her early pregnancy.

The phone vibrated on the glass coffee table, startling her. Ariel's name flashed across the screen, and Carly smiled, swiping to answer.

"Girl, you're back on the Gram!" Ariel's voice bubbled with excitement, cutting through the silence. "Look up the hashtag 'Charleston's It Couple,' and you'll see all the shots people took of you today. You're the shit, Carly. You looked stunning!"

Carly chuckled, her eyes drifting to the massive floor-to-ceiling windows where the Cooper River Bridge loomed in the distance, illuminated against the dark sky. "Slow your roll, Ariel." She placed the phone on speaker and rested it on the table, then leaned back and folded her arms over her stomach. "Weren't you supposed to be packing?"

"I am packing," Ariel shot back with a dramatic sigh. "I'm multitasking. Anyway, you looked like a boss today! I'm glad we booked that appointment with Tiana at Inner Glow Beauty. She killed your makeup. And those shoes from Hampden's? Killer. You totally broke them in, perfect for strutting in new outfits."

Carly laughed, shaking her head. "You're doing a lot of talking for someone who did the exact same thing. Don't act like you weren't turning heads too."

Ariel scoffed, but Carly heard the grin in her voice. "Sure, but everyone was calling your name, girl. 'Hey, Carly, look this way!' You were the star of the show."

Carly rolled her eyes but smiled. "Probably because of the promo for the Renovate Charleston event."

"Or maybe," Ariel teased, "because you're glowing, Mrs. Moore. Pregnancy looks amazing on you."

Carly's hand instinctively went to her belly again, her fingers pressing gently. "Maybe I look like I'm glowing, but the nausea says otherwise."

Ariel laughed softly. "Trust me, you're killing it. But hey, where's Mace?"

Carly's smile faltered slightly. She glanced at the door, willing it to open. "He's still not home. He promised he wouldn't be late, but… I think I'm just going to bed."

"Girl, you two are solid. Don't let his schedule get to you."

"I know." Carly sighed. "I'm trying not to let it."

She smiled softly, her eyes drifting to the large flat-screen TV on the wall. "Thanks, Ariel," she replied, shifting in her sheer black robe. The fabric barely covered the lace lingerie underneath, a secret she had kept for Mace. "But honestly, I'm exhausted. Today was a lot, and Mace still isn't home."

"Trust me, he knows what he has," Ariel assured her. "But hey, let me let you go. Rest up and give Mace a little surprise when he gets home. I'm sure you've got something up your sleeve—or under your robe."

Carly chuckled, shaking her head. "You know me too well."

"All right, talk to you later. Love you," Ariel said with a playful note before hanging up.

Carly looked up as the door clicked open. Her heart leaped when she heard Mace's familiar voice.

"Hey, babe," Mace called as he entered the room, his tall frame filling the doorway. "Sorry I'm late."

His words trailed off as his eyes drank her in. The low light from the city skyline highlighted her silhouette, the sheer robe clinging to her curves. He took his time entering the living room, his eyes glued to her as she rose from the couch. Carly reached for the remote, turning off the TV as her robe fluttered around her legs. She grabbed the front of it, but the thin fabric couldn't hide what she wore underneath—nothing much.

Mace's gaze darkened, and his throat bobbed as he swallowed hard. "I'm really sorry," he murmured, running a hand over his chest, trying to steady himself. His other hand moved lower to adjust his pants, struggling to conceal the evidence of his growing desire.

Carly arched an eyebrow, her lips curving into a knowing smile. "You said you'd be home in time for dinner," she reminded him, her voice soft but laced with subtle reproach. "It's in the fridge now. I think I'm going to bed."

But before she could turn away, Mace stepped forward, grabbing her hand gently. "Wait." He circled her, taking in every inch of her as though he hadn't seen her in years. "Sexy... yet alluring."

His fingers traced the edges of the lace bra peeking through her robe. His lips brushed the mounds of her breasts, and he inhaled deeply, savoring the faint scent of vanilla that clung to her skin. His hands untied the belt of her robe with ease, his gaze hungry as it fell open, revealing her thong beneath.

"Buttery-soft," he murmured as his fingers slid along the waistband before dipping lower, plunging into her wet heat.

"Mace..." Carly gasped, her knees weakening as she clutched his shoulders for support.

He grinned wickedly, withdrawing his finger and slipping it into his mouth, his eyes never leaving hers. "Yummy," he teased, his voice thick with desire. "I'm starving, Mrs. Moore. And I'll do anything if you let me eat all of you." He nibbled the delicate skin of her neck. "I meant, eat with me."

"Anything?" Carly's lips quirked as she placed a finger on her cheek. "You know, you never showed me those other dance moves you learned for the reception. You promised."

Mace raised a brow, his smile growing wider. "If you hadn't fallen asleep after I made love to you on our wedding night, you would've seen them." His tongue flicked over his lips, his eyes gleaming with mischief.

"Well," she purred, stepping closer and tugging on his tie, "this is as good a time as any. Do you need some music?"

She grabbed her phone, pulling up her playlist of sultry R&B tunes. The seductive beats filled the room, wrapping around them like a slow-burning fire.

Mace grinned as he loosened his tie, letting it fall to the floor. "Since you dressed up just for me, I won't disappoint."

He undid the buttons of his shirt with deliberate slowness, revealing the chiseled planes of his chest. His pants and shoes soon followed, leaving him in only his boxer briefs, his clothes puddled at his feet.

"Sit back," he ordered, his voice low and commanding.

Carly bit her lip, heat pooling in her belly as she obeyed, sinking into the couch. She raised one foot to rest on the cushion, the other planted on the floor, giving him a full view of her barely-there lingerie.

Mace's eyes darkened as he moved, his hips swaying to the rhythm of the music. His body rippled with every roll, each muscle flexing as he danced, his movements smooth and hypnotic.

"You want me, baby?" he whispered, his voice husky as he lowered himself, his abs tightening, his thighs flexing as he hovered inches away from her. His breath was warm on her skin, teasing her senses.

Carly's breath hitched, her pulse racing. "God, yes." Her fingers trailed down her chest, her touch igniting her skin as she watched him move.

Mace smirked, his body rolling with a slow sensuality that made her squirm. "You like that?" His lips ghosted over her knee as his hand slid up her thigh.

Carly's heart pounded, her desire building as he inched closer, his touch driving her mad with need. "You're my Magic Mace," she whispered, her voice barely audible over the pounding in her chest. "Take me."

He hovered over her, his hands bracketing her hips, his body taut with restraint. "I want to take you right here, but if I did," he growled, his voice rough with desire, "you wouldn't be able to walk to bed."

Carly let out a breathy laugh, her legs wrapping around his waist as she pulled him closer. "Who said I'm ready for bed?"

Mace's eyes gleamed as he scooped her up effortlessly, her legs still hooked around him. "Mrs. Moore, you're not getting much sleep tonight."

He carried her toward the bedroom, his muscles flexing beneath her touch. Carly's toes curled as her fingers dug into his back, feeling the power in every step he took.

"You've earned your supper," she whispered, her lips brushing against his ear.

"I plan on filling up," Mace shot back, his grin wicked. "And it's not just my stomach I'm talking about."

Her laughter turned into a gasp of pleasure as he pushed open the bedroom door and gently laid her on the bed. The music was replaced by the sounds of their moans as Mace made good on his promise.

"No one will ever destroy the paradise we've found," he whispered in her ear after their first round of lovemaking, his voice filled with unshakable certainty. "I won't let them."

Her phone buzzed after she placed it on the nightstand.

"Ignore it." Mace pushed it aside, his attention fully on her as he prepared to take her once more.

Carly's body responded instantly, melting into his as their world shrank down to nothing but their passion.

***

The following morning, the sun rose over the Cooper River, painting the horizon in strokes of yellowish orange. Its radiance seeped through the balcony doors, casting a soft glow over Mace and Carly as they sat under a throw blanket, nestled together on the love seat. The remnants of a light continental breakfast lay on the small table beside them, untouched by Carly, as they soaked in the tranquility of the morning.

"Isn't that the most gorgeous sunrise you've ever seen?" Carly asked, her voice soft as she gazed at Mace, the golden light reflecting in her eyes.

"If you say so." Mace chuckled, pulling her onto his lap. His arms circled around her waist as he leaned back, his legs resting on the table. "I'm usually in the office by now, but I have to admit, this day started better than yesterday. Well, your surprise visit was great… but what happened afterward, not so much."

Carly's fingers found the opening of his pajama shirt, tracing the soft, dark hair on his chest. She felt his steady heartbeat beneath her palm, grounding her. Mace's chin rested gently on the top of her head, his thumb grazing her arm.

"Tell me your thoughts," she whispered, tilting her head up for a kiss.

Mace hesitated, a deep sigh escaping his lips. "I was just wondering if you blamed me for this whole Nala mess."

Carly frowned, pulling back to look into his eyes. "Why would I blame you? Nala made her own choices, Mace. Besides, she's suing us, not just you."

"She's suing my company," he corrected, his voice low. "She blames me for ruining her life, but even knowing that, I wouldn't change what I did. I did it for you."

Her brow furrowed in confusion. "What do you mean?"

Mace ran a hand through his hair, frustration etched across his face. "I owed it to you. I knew you wanted a wedding with family and friends, but I couldn't wait anymore, Carly. I had already lost ten years with you, and I wasn't going to lose one more day. I needed to be your husband, needed it like I needed air. Even if it was just us, I had to make sure it happened."

He set her back on the love seat and walked to the balcony railing, his eyes scanning the harbor. Carly followed, her heart tugging as she saw the weight of his guilt and vulnerability. She pressed her body against his back, resting her cheek between his shoulder blades, feeling his frustration slowly melting under her touch.

"I understood that," she whispered, wrapping her arms around him. "I don't regret eloping. I wanted to marry you just as much as you wanted to marry me. Besides, Barbados was my idea, remember?"

Mace turned to face her, his eyes searching hers for reassurance. "But I rushed you. I took away the chance for your family to be there, for your aunt and brother to see you in your wedding dress."

Carly's throat tightened, but she forced a smile. "After my parents passed, I thought eloping would spare me the pain of their absence. But when we came home, I felt it anyway, the grief. It hit me like a tidal wave."

Mace's gaze softened as he tucked a stray lock of hair behind her ear. "I tried to make it special for you, even without them there. I wanted you to know I was thinking about them, especially your mother. That's why I made sure the room was filled with lilies… for her."

Tears welled in Carly's eyes. "I noticed. And the roses… the gardenias. Those were her favorites." She paused, swallowing the lump in her throat. "And the song… 'What a Wonderful World.' That was my parents' wedding song. How did you know?"

Mace's smile was bittersweet. "I didn't. It was a song my grandfather loved. I wanted to honor him too. I thought he'd appreciate being part of our day, just like your parents."

Carly leaned into him, her emotions swirling in a mixture of love, loss, and gratitude. She rested her forehead against his chest, her hand lingering over the spot where his heart was beating steadily. "Thank you for seeing me… for knowing me so well."

Mace kissed the top of her head. "I'll always know you, Carly. Every part of you."

They stood in silence, their connection palpable in the quiet of the morning. Finally, Carly broke the stillness, her voice lighter, as if the weight of the conversation had lifted.

"Are you going into the office today?"

"After lunch, maybe." He rubbed her back gently. "I'm more worried about you. You haven't been eating much, and I don't like the idea of you losing weight, especially now."

Carly sighed, her fingers tracing lazy circles on his chest. "The morning sickness usually passes, Mace. I'll be fine."

"You better be," he teased, lifting her chin with a gentle touch. "You promised you'd eat something, and I plan to hold you to that."

"I will." She smiled softly, leaning into him. "Yara is coming over later. We're going to spend the day together."

Mace groaned. "That Yara?"

Carly laughed, the sound light and melodic. "You sound just like Aunt Nora. She always calls her 'that Yara' too."

"Well, she's earned the title." He smirked, his hand wrapping possessively around her neck as he pulled her closer. "But I have a feeling today's going to be full of surprises."

Carly's eyes sparkled with mischief. "Good surprises, I hope."

Mace leaned in, brushing his lips against hers. "With you, they always are."

Chapter Four

THE training room buzzed with chatter as the Renovate Charleston community volunteers wrapped up their safety session.

Carly stepped forward, her voice clear and confident. "Thank you, Mr. Hunter, for the insightful training." She led the class in applause. "Safety on the building site is a priority, and we can't wait to assist with the renovations on the Westside." She beamed at the group before her, a mix of eager faces, some seasoned volunteers and others fresh to the cause.

Her phone buzzed on her desk. Carly glanced at it, a message from Yara lighting up the screen.

Yara: *Can I come in?*

Carly: *Y*

She hit Send quickly, her focus returning to the class as the door creaked open. Yara slipped in and took a seat in the back. Carly acknowledged her with a brief smile before addressing the group again.

"Remember"—Carly raised her hands to get everyone's attention—"you'll be provided with hard hats and goggles. Mr. Hunter recommended wearing jeans, a T-shirt, and closed-toe shoes. Thank you all for your commitment to this project."

She couldn't help but notice the array of designer handbags and high heels among the volunteers, a contrast to the casual attire recommended for a construction site. The long, flowing hair and high-end fashion screamed "Nala's entourage," though Nala herself was notably absent.

As the volunteers filed out, Carly caught Yara's eye. Yara, tall and effortlessly cool in her biker-chic outfit—dark-washed jeans, mini boots, and a leather jacket—looked entirely out of place yet perfectly at ease.

A delivery guy entered, sweat dripping down his brow. "Sorry I'm late, ma'am," he puffed, clearly out of breath. "There was an accident on the way here. I have an order for Professor Moore from Elsa's Eatery."

Carly frowned. "I didn't order anything." She pulled a small note from the bag. *Thanks for being a good customer, Elsa.*

"That's odd," Carly muttered, retrieving her wallet.

The delivery guy waved his hand. "It's already paid for. Tip included." He gave a nod before hurrying back out.

Carly raised an eyebrow, her suspicions piqued. Yara rolled her eyes dramatically, leaning over Carly's desk.

"You didn't order this food, so I don't trust it," Yara said, pushing away the bag. "Let's go out for lunch. This place smells like an over-perfumed department store." She wrinkled her nose. "And what's with all the designer heels at a safety training? Were those women auditioning for the *Real Housewives of Charleston*?"

Carly chuckled. "Nala Clarke's friends, no doubt. They're always dressed to impress."

Yara scoffed, her expression hardening. "I can't believe she's gained hundreds of thousands of followers just by announcing her lawsuit against Moore Investment Group."

"You were lurking on her social media?" Carly teased, tapping her chin.

"I call it research, professor." Yara grinned, her teasing tone softening.

Carly shook her head. "Well, Ariel's advice still stands—don't feed into Nala's drama. We don't work for her, and we certainly won't let her control our actions."

Yara linked her arm with Carly's, planting a kiss on her cheek. "Don't worry, sis. But remember, I'm your ride-or-die. I've got your back, even if it means stepping into some chaos."

As they left the office and headed to lunch in Park Circle, Carly reflected on Yara's fierce loyalty. The Park Circle area was lively, a mix of eclectic restaurants and stunning street art, with a small-town vibe that Carly loved. She and Mace had recently explored properties here for a potential new home. Carly felt an odd comfort returning to this familiar spot.

They settled at a wrought-iron table outside a small bistro, the smell of freshly brewed coffee and baked pastries wafting through the air. Yara, always quick to pull out her phone, showed Carly a post featuring a peppermint smoothie—the one Carly had ordered just last week.

"They call it the 'Baby M.'" Yara snickered. "Looks like someone overheard you talking about how peppermint helps with your morning sickness. 'M' as in Moore."

Carly groaned, her hand instinctively resting on her baby bump. "I feel so violated."

"Get used to it." Yara shrugged. "Life in the land of income with six to nine zeros means people are always watching." Before Carly could respond, Yara's gaze sharpened. "Look to the side, there's a man heading toward us."

Carly's pulse quickened as Yara's hand subtly moved to her concealed holster. "Yara, don't. Not here."

Yara remained silent, her eyes locked on the approaching man.

"Hi," he said, his hands raised in a peaceful gesture. "I don't mean to intrude—"

Before he could finish, Nala appeared, storming toward the table. "Preston! You're supposed to stay thirty feet away from me," she barked, drawing the attention of nearby patrons.

Carly's heart sank. *Not again.*

"Is this the fiancé?" Yara asked, focused on Carly, barely acknowledging Nala.

Carly replied quietly, "Yara, please don't."

Nala's eyes darted between Yara and Carly. "Are you Carly's bodyguard or something?"

Yara leaned back, her voice calm but dangerous. "I suggest you both take this little soap opera elsewhere."

Nala didn't budge. "I'm not leaving until he does."

"I just wanted to introduce myself," Preston said, backing away slowly and apologizing as he left the scene.

Carly, feeling the hostility build, tried to diffuse the situation. "Nala, this isn't the place for this. Please, leave."

Nala's face twisted into a smirk. "Carly, I'll see you at the Renovate Charleston event," she spat before turning on her heel and strutting away.

Yara remained unfazed, tapping her fingers on the table.

Carly let out a long breath, finally able to relax. "Did Mace ask you to be my bodyguard, Yara?"

Yara's lips curled into a smile. "He didn't have to. You know I've got your back."

"Yeah, I know. But maybe let's not antagonize the tiger next time."

Yara laughed, her eyes twinkling with mischief. "Tiger? Nala's a house cat with good PR."

"She's a tiger nonetheless." Carly raised her hand to get the attention of their waiter.

"Ma'am, your bill has been settled." He smiled. "Your charges were added to your husband's corporate account. Have a great day." He backed away and ended their discussion.

"I told you the air was different in the land of many zeroes," Yara said.

"I'll need to talk to Mason." She grabbed her bag and rose from her seat.

"What do you plan to say to him?" She snickered. "'Honey, stop spending your millions on me.'"

Carly stood there staring at Yara. "Give me the keys. I'm driving this time."

"Oh…" Yara looked down at her hands. "I know I'm in trouble when you don't let me play with your toys."

Carly side-eyed Yara. "Stop it, girl. This is serious."

Chapter Five

CARLY slid into her black Audi R8, the engine purring to life, a gift from Mace after their Barbados trip. She glanced at Yara, who sat rigid in the passenger seat as they merged onto Interstate 26. The friction between them crackled like static electricity. She turned her attention to the road, her knuckles whitening around the steering wheel. "What the hell was that with Preston and Nala? Mace must have told you something. Reaching for your gun? What's going on?"

Yara shifted uncomfortably, her gaze fixed out the window. "What are you talking about?"

Carly shot her a glance. "Did Mace put you up to this? Encouraging you to antagonize Nala like that?" She couldn't shake the nagging suspicion that Mace's influence had stretched further than she realized.

"No!" Yara's response was sharp, her chest rising and falling as she struggled to keep her composure.

"Don't let Mace and his money change you… change us. I love my husband, but I know how he uses it to ensure the outcome is in his favor. He can be quite persuasive." Carly's voice was calm, but her eyes darted to Yara, searching for a hint of understanding.

Yara's expression tightened, pain flickering behind her eyes. "After all these years, that's what you're thinking? We've been through too much, Carly." Her voice wavered, tears welling as she blinked rapidly.

"For the record, I have a contract with Mace's company, but he doesn't control me." Her voice dropped, vulnerability seeping through her words. "Do you think I did that because… because I'm more loyal to him than you?" She turned to Carly, tears streaming down her cheeks now, her lips trembling. "Is that what you're getting at?"

Carly's heart squeezed at the sight of her friend's pain, but she pressed on. "No. I'm not worried about that."

She pulled the car over, shifting into park. This conversation couldn't be had while navigating the highway.

Yara wiped her tears with the back of her hand. "Then what? What are we talking about here?"

The vulnerability in Yara's eyes made Carly's chest ache. They'd been through thick and thin together, but something had shifted. And Carly had to face it head-on.

"We've always been honest with each other," Carly said softly, turning to fully face Yara. She took Yara's hand, the physical connection grounding her. "I feel like I can't tell you everything anymore."

Yara's eyes widened, shock mingling with sadness. "That's not true. Carly, I've always been there for you. I just… I don't tell you every ratchet thing I do." She gave a weak smile, trying to lighten the mood.

Carly's lips twitched, but the heaviness in her chest remained. "That's not what I mean. It's about Mace. I've seen how you and Ariel react around him." She let out a breath, loosening her grip on Yara's hand and rubbing her temples. "I'm starting to feel like Mace is everywhere in my life, pulling strings."

Yara leaned back in her seat, her hands falling to her lap. "Carly… I didn't realize you felt that way. But you're not exactly innocent either. You're the one who eloped with Mace, the one who chose to stay here, in Charleston, for him. You've made sacrifices too. You gave up your position at the college in Maryland. We're not the only ones under his spell."

Carly's breath caught in her throat. She hadn't expected her friend to call her out so directly, but she couldn't deny the truth in what Yara was saying.

"You're right," Carly whispered, her fingers trembling as she placed her hand back on Yara's. "I've been so caught up in this whirlwind with Mace."

Yara's lips pressed together as she gave a small nod. "We're still here for you, Carly. Ariel and I—we'll always be here *for you.* But don't worry, we've all got our own limits too."

Carly felt the weight of her friend's words. She exhaled slowly, her shoulders sinking under the burden of unspoken truths. "I need to talk to him. Really talk to him."

Yara's lips curved into a soft smile. "Yeah, maybe that's a good idea." She wiped away the remnants of her tears. "Enough heavy talk for one day. Let's go pick up those outfits you ordered and do something fun."

Carly's chest loosened as the stress eased between them. She hovered her finger over the car's start button, glancing sideways at Yara. "Are we good?"

Yara's grin broke the last of the tension. "We're good, Peppermint Patty. But seriously, you've been chugging those smoothies like there's no tomorrow."

They both burst into laughter, the strain of their conversation melting away for the moment. As Yara pulled out her phone, she flashed Carly the screen, showing Nala sipping a drink at a nearby restaurant. "Round two of Nala vs. Peppermint Patty?"

Carly rolled her eyes with a grin. "Bananas." She pressed the start button, the car roaring back to life, and they headed off.

Carly dropped Yara off before heading home, their bond repaired. Once home, she slipped inside, her shopping bags in hand, and headed straight to the mirror. Her all-black ensemble, complete with the edgy makeup Yara had convinced her to try, gave her a confidence she hadn't felt in a long time.

But when she heard Mace's voice behind the closed dining room door, her pulse quickened. She pushed the door open, freezing at the sight before her.

Mace stood at the head of the table, a large screen behind him displaying graphs and figures. Around the table sat his executive team, each man dressed sharply in a black suit, their gazes now fixed on her, jaws dropping.

She hadn't expected this.

"I didn't realize you had company," she murmured, her eyes darting from Mace to the suited men.

Mace's gaze roamed over her, his expression morphing from surprise to admiration, a slow smile curving his lips.

One of the men leaned over to his colleague and whispered, "She's hot..."

Mace's sharp response cut him off. "I can hear you."

His attention returned to Carly, and as he walked toward her, his lidded eyes and easy swagger sent a rush of heat through her.

"What are you trying to do to me?" Mace murmured, leaning in close, his breath hot against her ear. "You're making me lose focus."

She smirked, whispering back, "I didn't know we had company. I need to talk to you afterward."

Mace's gaze swept down her body, lingering on her legs and the new boots. "You look incredible." He kissed both sides of her lips, sending a spark through her. "Of course, we can talk. You have my full attention." Turning to his team, Mace's voice became firm. "Gentlemen, that's it for tonight. We'll pick this up tomorrow."

The men shuffled out as Mace took Carly's hand, his eyes locked on hers, his voice a low, seductive growl. "Now, let's *talk*."

With a sly smile, Mace guided her to the bedroom for their evening discussion. *Stay focused*, Carly reminded herself. She knew that look. Mace had other things on his mind.

***

Mace's heart pounded as he nudged Carly, her soft breathing the only sound in the room. "Babe, it's your phone," he whispered.

She didn't stir; her body cocooned under the covers. The phone rang again, piercing the quiet with a persistent, unfamiliar ringtone. He groaned, frustration building. Rubbing his hand across his face, he sat up, the pressure in his chest mounting.

"Carly, your phone's been ringing for minutes." His voice, edged with impatience, softened as his gaze settled on her warm, cocoa-brown skin. Even in moments like this, her beauty stirred something primal in him, something protective. He leaned over, brushing a hand down her back. "Babe, wake up."

"What?" Carly blinked, her voice husky from sleep. "What's going on?"

"Your phone." He pointed at the glowing device on the nightstand, his jaw tightening. "Someone's really trying to get ahold of you." His desire to pull her back into bed warred with the growing sense that whatever was happening wasn't just an inconvenience.

She sighed, reaching for the phone. "It's Yara," she murmured, her gaze drifting over Mace's body, but he could see the shift in her expression.

"Answer it," he said, trying to keep the rising tightness out of his voice as he headed to the bathroom, his movements brisk, purposeful. His unease spiked when he heard Carly's voice behind him, wavering, uncertain.

"You're calling this late to tell me to turn on the news?" Carly's tone had sharpened, her earlier languor gone. Mace froze, gripping the doorframe as he caught a glimpse of her furrowed brow. "Yara, what's so urgent that it can't wait until morning?"

There was a long pause. The air felt heavy, charged with something unsaid. Mace clenched his fists. He didn't like this. He knew Carly and her girls had a bond he respected, but this? Late-night calls, hushed tones—something was wrong.

"Mace," Carly's voice trembled as she hung up the phone, "turn on the TV. Yara said there's something we need to see."

His pulse quickened. "Carly..." The impatience in his voice now barely masked his worry.

He grabbed the remote, turning on the news, the glow of the screen casting an eerie light over the room. When he crawled back into bed, she curled up beside him. He pulled her close, his protective instincts kicking in. His mind raced as the report unfolded.

"Breaking news," the anchor's voice, jarring and emotionless, cut through the quiet. "Brandon Cross, a former student and new building management employee at the university, has been found dead in his home."

Mace stiffened. He felt Carly tense against him, her hand covering her mouth in shock.

"Brandon…?" she whispered.

The reporter continued, describing the scene of food spilled on the floor, a half-eaten sandwich, a bag in his hand. But it was the next detail that sent chills down Mace's spine. "Here's footage showing Brandon leaving Professor Carly Moore's classroom with the same bag just before his death."

Carly's sob was like a knife twisting in Mace's chest. "That's… that's the lunch that I got but didn't order today."

His mind raced. *How had Brandon ended up with her lunch?* And worse, what if she had eaten it? He turned, gripping her shoulders, his voice strained. "Carly, did you eat any of it? Should we go to the hospital? What if…?"

Her wide eyes locked with his. "No. No, I didn't. Yara came before I could. The delivery guy… I didn't recognize him. It wasn't the usual person."

His heart slammed against his ribs. *This wasn't an accident.* He pulled Carly into him, his arms tightening around her, as if holding her could protect her from whatever danger had seeped into their lives. He pressed his lips to her hair, the smell of her calming him even as his mind raced to dark places he didn't want to go. *Who would want to hurt her or their unborn child?*

His body tensed, every muscle taut with dread and fury simmering beneath the surface. He had enemies. He had made them over the years, clawing his way to the top of a cutthroat world, but Carly? She was innocent, caught in the crossfire of a world she hadn't asked to be a part of. He couldn't lose her. He wouldn't.

"You're safe," Mace whispered, even as his mind screamed otherwise. "You and the baby, you're both safe." He pressed his hands over her stomach, the need to shield her overwhelming him. His jaw clenched, his breath shallow. He had no idea who was behind this, but they had made the worst mistake of their life.

Carly sniffed, nodding, but the fear in her eyes wouldn't fade. "I'll give my statement tomorrow at the police station," she whispered.

"We'll go together," Mace replied, his voice hard, unyielding. "We're handling this together."

She trembled in his arms. "I feel so sorry for Brandon's mother. I can't imagine… losing a child…" She closed her eyes, but it didn't stop the tears falling that wet Mace's chest and tightened the pull on his heart.

"I'm here for you," he whispered in her ear.

Her breathing, calm but uneven, kept him awake. He wanted to take some of her pain away, feelings that he knew had escaped from a place she had kept buried for a long time. When she finally fell asleep, Mace's heart constricted. He stroked her hair, his thoughts spiraling to the countless times he had heard the whispers of Carly's past. She'd lost so much, more than anyone should have to bear. He held her tighter, his heart aching for her. As her breathing slowed, he heard her mumble in her sleep.

"I'm sorry, Lilly… I'm so sorry," she uttered from somewhere in her dreams. "Mommy is so sorry I couldn't save you."

Mace froze. Lilly. He didn't know who Lilly was, but the name felt heavy, steeped in a grief he hadn't been privy to.

"It's okay." He placed kisses on her cheek. She stirred but didn't awaken. "Who's Lilly?"

He looked at her, but she had quieted down. Her heart wouldn't reveal any more of her secrets.

Whoever Lilly was, it was another part of Carly's soul he was determined to protect, no matter what the cost.

Chapter Six

CARLY reported to work after giving her statement at the police department that morning. Her classroom and office had been relocated to different locations as both were considered parts of an ongoing investigation. Black and yellow police crime tape covered the locked doors. Despite her requests, she was not allowed to go into her office or former classroom to retrieve her things.

Carly, dressed in traditional business attire, surveyed the classroom overflowing with students who had come for their final instructions prior to the Renovate Charleston Community Service project. “Thanks, Sam, for the safety lecture before we go onsite with the community project. Are there any more question?”

Sam Peterson was a project manager on many of the local projects undertaken by Mace’s company, Moore Investment Group. He had agreed to help the students understand the importance of following safety procedures on any construction site.

One of the students raised their hand. “What do you think about what happened last night?”

Sam began collecting his things. “I guess that’s my cue to leave since there are no questions for me.”

He waved goodbye to Carly, who waved back but was silent as she contemplated her answer. She removed her glasses from the bridge of her nose.

"I believe she was referring to questions about the renovation," Sam noted before he walked out.

More hands went in the air before Carly's response.

"I can't comment on an ongoing investigation," she told them as she quickly decided it was best to settle the brewing curiosity by not elaborating on the news about Brandon. The hands went down like air escaping and deflating a balloon.

"I knew Brandon," one of the students commented to another.

"He didn't deserve what happened to him," came the response of another student. "He was turning his life around."

Carly was about to comment again, signaling an end to the class, when a collective gasp came—from mainly the female students. She looked at the door with a window carved into it to see what had commanded their attention.

Mace. There he stood, looking at her through the window.

After they had left the police station, Mace told her he had to attend a meeting downtown on Broad Street. He didn't mention that he would be dropping by her classroom. Looking every bit the part of a captain of industry, one in charge of his own fate, he turned the knob and stood in the doorway in one of his black Tom Ford suits, the one that always claimed attention when he entered the room.

"Please don't let me interrupt." He stood in the doorway until Carly gave him permission to enter the room.

"Come on in."

Of course you're interrupting. She mused and allowed a small smile to form on her lips. Unlike when she discovered Nala checking out her man the morning she stormed into his office, she wasn't angry that most of the students and volunteers looked at him with a mixture of lust and dreamy desire.

"Are you Mr. Moore?" one of her students asked him. "The Mason Moore?"

He nodded, standing in full view of the class in his classic cut suit. The suit had been custom-made for him with its suspended waist and wide lapels. It had been ten years since his college years, but the man could still win any competition against men in their prime. The shoulder of his jacket was broad, giving him a strong silhouette, and his trousers fit his trim physique.

"I'll just sit in the back." He ascended the stairs with heads turning as he approached each row.

Before he found his seat, Yara came in dressed like a typical college coed in jeans and a white T-shirt. She waved at Carly before finding a seat beside Mace.

"Let's adjourn for now," Carly said to the class. "You all have successfully completed the safety course before we go onsite. Don't forget to turn in your research paper about one of the historic neighborhoods in Charleston."

A collective groan filled the room.

Mace raised his hand, silencing the complaints. "I've been impressed at how all of you have embraced this project. As a stakeholder in maintaining the charm and history of Charleston, I'd like to reward all of you with a celebration."

Cheers rang throughout the room.

"Maybe a big party like a masquerade party? The location and date to be determined?" He smiled in response to the applause.

"What are you doing?" Carly mouthed to him, cocking her head.

"Thanks, man!" A student high-fived him. "Can we bring a plus-one?"

"Sure thing." He stood before them. "I'll have one of my assistants get your information when you all come to the project next week."

They filed out of the room, leaving only Mace and Yara with Carly.

"What was that?" Carly furrowed her brow.

"You have a problem with giving a reward to your students?" He placed a hand under his chin. "I just thought that since all of you have worked hard on this project, a little fun afterward would be a good thing."

"It would have been nice if we discussed it first." She opened the drawer of her desk and pulled out her pocketbook.

Yara cleared her throat. "I think she was asking the real reason for the party." She placed a fist to her mouth and widened her eyes.

Carly tightened her lips, awaiting his answer.

"If you insist, but plausible deniability would be best." He placed his hands behind his back. "One of your students may have information about Brandon and what happened to him. I plan to place my men in the crowd to listen out for information. Anyone who messes with my wife and child…" He paused as his mood darkened. "They mess with me, and they will regret it."

Carly came around the desk and placed a hand on his cheek. "Don't you think we should let the authorities handle this?" She gazed into his eyes. "I want to know what happened also, but I don't want to hinder the investigation."

"I promise I won't get in the way." He placed an arm around her waist.

"Good." She smiled and kissed him. "Was there another reason you came here? You told me you have a very busy day today."

"You know I have to check on my girl." He smiled that lopsided smile that she'd fallen in love with so many years ago. "It's what I do."

She giggled. "Your girl is fine. Do you want to go to lunch with me and Yara?"

"I'll have to take a rain check." He loosened his embrace. "Now that I know you're all right, I can get back to work." Leaning forward, he kissed her, then waved at Yara. "Have fun and try to stay out of trouble." He chuckled before heading for the door.

"Oh, I almost forgot." He made a half-turn, pivoting on one foot and showing his Italian leather shoes, polished to perfection. "Yara, Carly told me how much you admired her car, but you preferred one of the newer Lexus sport models."

"Yes, but with my current technology support contracts, I'm going to need a little more coin." Yara snorted and placed her hands on her hips.

Mace reached into his pocket, grabbing something that sounded like metal on metal. "Catch." He tossed a set of keys with the luxury brand logo. "Happy birthday."

Yara caught the keys midair. "But it's not my birthday."

"As sure as you're breathing, sis, you either have already had a birthday this year or will have a birthday. Enjoy."

Yara covered her mouth with her hand and did a happy dance before leaping toward Carly for a full embrace. "Did you know about this?" Tears ran down her cheeks.

"No." Carly looked at Mace. "My man is full of surprises today."

Yara released Carly and, with her hands flapping in the air, hugged Carly again before running to hug Mace. "No one has ever been this generous to me before." She covered her face with her hands as she stood in front of him. "I don't know if I should keep this. It's too much. How could I ever repay you?"

Mace placed his hands firmly on her shoulders and looked into her eyes. "You're a sister to Carly, and that makes you like a sister to me. I would be offended if you didn't accept my gift. Family is supposed to be here for each other. I'm blessed that I could meet your need."

Yara looked at Carly, who nodded.

"Enjoy. It's parked in the reserved parking lot, space 225." He smiled at Yara and blew a kiss to Carly, who had taken her phone out of her pocketbook. "See you at home. I love you." He waved goodbye.

"I love you too." She blew him a kiss and waited until he had exited her office before she hit Send on the message she finished typing.

We need to talk. She heard the familiar buzz of his phone outside the door.

Message received. He replied.

"Ready to go?" Carly asked while gathering her things as she turned to face Yara, who was still bouncing on air.

"Is he always this generous?" Yara locked arms with Carly.

"He is a generous man, and I love him, but, Yara, you know people don't give expensive things without conditions."

"I'll keep that in mind." She grabbed Carly's hand. "Let's go see my new toy."

***

"Carly, please tell Mace how much I love this car." Yara smiled, dancing in her seat to a familiar tune on the radio. "Oh, that's my jam."

She looked at the traffic gathering on the highway as they made their way from the restaurant downtown and an afternoon of shopping before they headed to the northern side of the city. She maneuvered her new Lexus sports car like a pro, leaning back in her plush leather seat as she looked at the tech screen with navigation and the newest safety features.

"I'm glad we had time to spend another day together." Carly looked at her friend above the lens of her designer shades. "I was surprised you agreed to lunch. I know you're busy."

"Not too busy to check on a friend." She looked at Carly with soft brown eyes filled with concern. "I knew it was hard for you to hear the sorrow of another woman who has to deal with the loss of a child. Brandon was an adult, but seeing the anguish on his mother's face as she looked into the camera and pleaded for anyone to come forward broke my heart. I know you, girl, and although a lot has happened since your miscarriage years ago, a little light in your eyes has dimmed since the loss. I wanted to make sure you were all right."

Carly placed a hand on Yara's hand resting on the shift lever. "You know me, and yes, it was hard hearing another woman cry over losing her child. The pain gets easier to bear with time, but it never goes away." Carly rubbed her growing belly with the other hand. "You just learn to live with it."

They both looked out the window at the passing scenery.

Carly smiled and broke the growing silence. "Time also brings on new joys and new experiences. We're both examples of surviving the hard times." She took a deep breath. "Thanks for coming with me to visit the Clarke Store. They specialize in Bajan imports. I've been meaning to visit the place since returning from Barbados. I hear they have authentic jewelry and pottery imported from that country. I want to collect a few pieces since Mace and I got married there."

Yara maneuvered the car into a space on the street as close as they could get to the entrance to the store. "I've gotten all the new things I need for one day, but I'm glad to go shopping with you." She placed the car in park and cut the engine. "Let's go. This is shaping up to be a great day."

Carly and Yara entered the store filled mainly with silver metal shelves of pottery, all with vibrant palettes of colors of earth and sky. At the other end of the store were display cases containing diamond, gold, and sterling jewelry. A sign above one of the cases identified the pieces as unique and crafted by artists from coconut shells, coral, and threaded beads used to create stunning necklaces, earrings, and bracelets. They looked around as they walked to the center of the store containing wall-to-wall items.

"That's gorgeous." Carly pointed at a collection of vases and functional tableware accented with cobalt blue that was both eye-catching and brilliant in colors. "This pattern reminds me of sunrays and the peaceful Bajan sunsets."

She moved closer to the pieces and took a plate off the shelf to get a closer look at it. Turning the plate over, she noticed something she hadn't seen on the back of the handcrafted pottery made by the local artists in Barbados. She frowned as she looked at another plate, a vase, and several bowls all containing the unfamiliar mark on the underside of the pottery.

"This is odd." She motioned to Yara, who was less than three feet in front of her. "I don't recall seeing these marks in any of the pottery shops I visited on the island."

She showed Yara the dark brown marks with one-inch horizontal lines covered with one-half inch vertical lines in a basketweave pattern on all the pottery they turned over to observe.

"It's not odd." They turned to look at Nala approaching them, followed by a tabby cat with green eyes hissing at them. "Stop it, Misty," she reprimanded the cat. "We need to welcome our guests."

Yara tilted her head back and rolled her eyes. "It is odd that you're here. We run into you yet again." She paused, giving voice to her frustration. "Can we go anywhere without *poof,* you magically appearing?" She raised her hand and used her index finger as if she was waving a magic wand. "You remember how you told your ex that it was uncomfortable *bumping* into him at the restaurant a few days ago? Well, I'm getting the same strange vibes."

Carly moved between Yara and Nala. "It's a… surprise seeing you here since you weren't at the safety session earlier. It was important that each participant in the Renovate Charleston project attend." Carly crossed her arms.

"You didn't say it was mandatory." Nala shifted her body in a defensive stance. "I needed to post content for my *millions* of followers on social media. Did I tell you how much my sites have grown since I filed a suit against Moore Investment Group?" She looked at her fingers and flipped away imaginary dirt under her well-manicured French tips.

Carly flinched, more from the weight settling in her chest at the reminder of Mace's company being sued than Yara bumping up against her, trying to confront Nala. Carly held her back, pushing Yara away.

"After I finished posting, Simeon said he needed me at the store." Nala rubbed her temple. "I'm beginning to think that you all are following me." She cupped her hand around her mouth and turned her head toward the back of the store. "Cassidy, where are you? We have customers."

"I'm busy doing what Simeon told me to do. Inventory," a voice called back.

Nala rolled her eyes, then leaned around Carly to look at Yara taking pictures of the store. "Please, we ask that no flash photography is taken."

Yara looked at the various signs posted in calligraphy noting that the pottery was all authentic and made of red clay from Barbados. "I don't see anything saying we can't take pictures before we decide to make purchases. Do you, Carly?" Yara placed her phone in the back pocket of her jeans.

"No, I don't either." Carly shook her head while walking around the aisle and taking pictures of the unusual marking on the backs of several pieces. "Is the owner available? I have some questions."

Nala tightened her lips. "You can ask me any question you may have." She pushed several of the vases closer to the wall. "My family, the Clarkes, own this place. Actually, it's my brother, Simeon, who owns the place." Nala's eyes darted around the room. Carly noticed that her voice increased in volume. "He's not here."

"Well, I'd like to leave my card." Carly reached into her cross-body bag and pulled out a card, *Dr. Carly Rivers Moore. Professor of History* that contained her contact information and handed it to Nala. "I guess we'll be leaving."

Another customer came in through the door, shifting their attention away from questions about the pottery.

"Welcome to the Clarke Store." Nala smiled brightly at the woman looking around. She turned back to Carly, extending her hand toward the door. "I helped my parents renovate this building and I'm familiar with safety features. I'm looking forward to participating in the project. If you'll check the site, you'll see that all the buzz *I* created has increased the donations for it tenfold." She smiled before walking away to answer the new customer's questions. "You're welcome, Dr. Moore."

"I've got to give it to her. That bitch has got some nerve." Yara placed her hand through the bend in Carly's arm and pulled Carly toward the door.

Planting her feet, Carly remained still as she looked around the store. "Maybe it's the nerve that it takes to hide something."

The sun was setting when they left the store and walked the short distance back to the car, past the line of boutique shops with staff preparing for closing time. Large pots containing greenery lined the street that had been filled with visitors and customers.

Yara used her key to unlock the car before she looked both ways and walked to the driver's side. While Carly waited to enter the passenger side, her phone buzzed, and she took the phone with its bejeweled case out of her pocketbook.

A car's horn, fast approaching, blared. Yara tried to flatten her body against her vehicle as the car roared down the street too close for comfort. Before she could get out of the way, the car stopped alongside her. The doors of the backseat flew open, and two men jumped out. One pushed Yara to the ground and held her down despite her flailing her arms and kicking her feet. They took her phone out of her jeans pocket.

Carly's heart raced. Sweating from all pores, with every nerve in her body frantically firing, she wasn't aware of the man running toward her before he grabbed her by the back of the shirt and stopped her from going to help Yara.

"Stop. Please." Carly screamed, "Don't harm us. I'm pregnant. Take whatever you want." Her breath quickened as she negotiated with her attacker.

"Give me your phone. Now," he said in a hostile voice. He grabbed the phone out of her hand then pushed her against the car.

One of the men who had subdued Yara slapped her in the face. "Let's get out of here."

They all got in a dark car with the license plate removed and sped away before others stuck their heads out of the doors in response to Yara and Carly's screams.

"Yara, are you all right?" Carly rushed to her side, crying as she rocked Yara in her arms. Her legs were weak, but she knew they needed to get out of the road.

"I'm okay." Yara leaned against the car to avoid placing her weight on Carly as they rose to their feet. Carly maintained her balance while providing a brace for Yara.

"Calm down." Carly fought back her fears as she held her stomach to soothe the cramping that had started when she saw Yara go down and was getting worse.

Chapter Seven

THE door swung open before Carly could place her key in the door of the condo. Mace stood in front of her dressed in a T-shirt and pajama pants. He moved to the side to allow her entrance into the foyer. As much as he tried to avoid scowling, his brows furrowed as he spewed questions peppered with frustration.

"Where were you?" He moved to face her. "I've been trying to call you for the past hour." He placed his hands on his hips. "Hell, maybe for the last two hours." He ran his hands through his hair and turned his face to the wall, giving himself a few seconds to measure his tone and keep his volume in check. He placed his hand with a little pressure on her shoulder while bombarding her with questions. "Why didn't you answer your phone?"

"I lost my phone." She stopped in her tracks and glared at him.

"I tried calling Yara too, and she didn't answer." He came closer and placed both hands on her shoulders.

"She… she lost her phone too," she stammered. "That's not entirely true. The phones were taken from us." She maneuvered around him and walked in.

"I don't understand." He picked up his pace to run in front of her. "I don't understand why we're in a face-off." His heart pounded. "Please make this make sense. Tell me something… anything."

She backed away, her eyes moistening with tears. "Am I going to have to face an interrogation with you? Now?" She threw her bag on the couch and rubbed her stomach. "I'm sorry I didn't call you, but my phone was taken away from me during an attack on me and Yara. This has not been a good day."

Attack. His head snapped back, and he was stunned by her words. His blood heated and a sheen of sweat appeared on his brow. He lowered his head and moved toward the couch to comfort Carly, who had turned away from him.

Taking her into his arms, he let his need to protect her from harm overshadow the fear he had experienced in her absence. "Babe, I was worried about you and the baby." He placed his chin on the top of her head and rubbed her arms. "You're safe now, and you don't have to answer any more questions right now. We can talk in the morning if you want to." He took her hands and noticed that the skin on her fingers was red and inflamed. "What?" His breath caught, and he closed his mouth. *No more questions.*

"It's not painful." She looked into his eyes while he focused on her hands. "My phone was snatched out of my hand and the crystals on the case scratched my skin. The man who took my phone grabbed me by the collar, forcing my back against the door of the car."

Mace narrowed his eyes, and his vision blurred, colored red. He slowly raised her hand to his lips, kissing her fingers tenderly. "I'm sorry I wasn't there to protect you." His lips tightened. "You asked me to go to lunch with you and I chose to go to a meeting instead." He tightened his arms around her and slid her on his lap. "That decision could have cost you your life." He snuggled her close to his chest. "I wouldn't have been able to live with myself if something had happened to you or the baby."

"I don't blame you for what happened any more than you could blame me."

"I don't blame you," he said quickly. He looked deep into her eyes, hoping she saw he spoke with a truth that was soul deep. "I blame the ass who was stupid enough to attack you."

"He shook me up but..." She looked off into space. "I can't help but wonder why they did it. Two guys were fighting with Yara. They were rougher on her, like... like there was something personal about this attack. They threw her down on the ground." She choked and placed a hand to her face. "They threw her down and slapped her in the face."

He clenched his jaw, and his arm muscles tightened.

"Finally, a few people who were in the stores heard us screaming and called the police. We gave a statement before we went to the emergency room. I should have had someone notify you, but for the last few days, you've been coming home late. I thought I would be home before you and I was focused on getting help for Yara and getting the baby checked out. Things happened so fast, Mace. I'm sorry you were worried. It's just that nothing like this has ever happened to me before. I handled it the best I could."

He rubbed her back, then her belly. "Is the baby, okay?"

He examined her eyes then raised her shirt, looking for anything that may have signaled their unborn child had been caught up in the nightmare.

"Our obstetrician met me at the emergency room." She placed a reassuring hand on his resting on her belly. "She said the baby is all right. The cramping I was experiencing was probably from all the adrenaline running through my body. She didn't place me on any precautions. She said I was fine, just shaken up."

"So, it's important that you remain calm." He buried his lips in his mouth.

"Yes, and I'm getting there now that I know Yara is okay. My cousin Daniel was in town visiting Aunt Nora. He came over to the emergency room and brought us home."

The muscles around his mouth tightened. "You called Daniel? Not me?"

She turned to straddle his lap. "No, babe." She shook her head. "Yara told the nurse to call Daniel. She had visited Aunt Nora earlier in the day and knew he was in town. The two of them have been friends for years. Aunt Nora has always treated Yara like family." She placed her hands on the sides of his face. "Like I said, I thought you were at the office."

"I heard you." He bit his lip. "I guess we'll need time for me to prove where my priorities are. My business deals don't come before you. I hope you'll someday believe that." His mouth slackened as he bent his neck forward, touching his forehead to hers.

"It's not you, really… it's me." She placed a chaste kiss on his lips. "I've been on my own for so long that I mistakenly thought it was on me to solve this problem. I ask for your patience as I show *you* that I know it's about us. We're family, for better or worse."

"I had planned a peaceful evening for us." A bitter smile covered his face. "I wanted to make it a special surprise."

"What did you plan?" She tilted her head. "I could use something special."

"Really?" A sweet smile covered his face. "Come with me." He led her to the back of the condo, where a closed door was covered with a red ribbon. "Surprise."

She looked up at him.

"Go ahead." He extended his hand. "See what's inside."

She tore down the ribbon and turned the knob. Behind the closed door was a room—which had once been filled with exercise equipment—transformed into an oasis of tranquility.

"Oh my gosh," she squealed, covering her mouth with her hand. "What did you do?"

"Do you like it?" His face brightened.

Carly walked into the space. One wall was covered with stone with a bench in front of it. On top of the bench was a black silk bikini lying on a robe with soft, fluffy slippers on the floor. Lush greenery was placed on both sides of the bench near the wall. Low lights helped to create a Zen feel.

"I thought you said you were going to turn this into a media room for your tech equipment." Carly looked back at him smiling and still standing in the doorway.

He chuckled. "I lied. My bad." He came closer and stood beside her. "I always had it in mind to change this into a space where you felt relaxed and cared for." He took her into his arms, kissing her along the angle of her jaw down to the sensitive skin along her neck.

"Thank you, but I don't doubt you love me."

She opened her mouth to receive the attention he greedily lavished upon her. The warmth of her smooth, silken lips, the tenderness of the walls of her mouth, and the way that her tongue, darting in and out, teased him before claiming him always turned him on. Electricity surged through his body, igniting every nerve and heating his manhood with desire. He would build a kingdom for her and be her willing servant. Yes, he loved her, and he wanted to make sure nothing and no one would ever make her question it.

"The windows to this room are on the west side of our place." He released her from his embrace and walked before her toward the windows. "I thought we would be spending the evening watching the sun set together." He didn't hide his disappointment.

"I'm happy to watch the starry sky with you." She stood in front of the window. "It's a wonderful night. I think we both deserve the peace of observing nature. I've loved looking at the sky since I was a little girl—the beauty of the clouds, the colorful display of the sunrise and the sunset with its orange, yellow and pink ribbons." She swayed as he came behind her and looked out the window.

"I remember how as kids, our friends would be busy playing, but you… you preferred to lie on the grass on your back and look up at the clouds."

"Sometimes, you joined me," she recalled, laughing. "We would imagine what shapes were in the clouds."

"Not because I loved cloud watching." He placed a lock of her curly hair behind her ear. "It's because I wanted to spend time with you."

"That's sweet." She turned to face him, warm brown eyes looking into his piercing orbs.

"Keeping you in my thoughts has been part of my survival," he spoke in low tones, his lips to her ear. "I've been successful in business, but the past ten years without you have cost me a lot. I knew my soul was dying. I could feel it. In your absence, money became a pale substitute for the joy I'd felt with you." He lowered his head and swallowed the lump in his throat. Gathering strength to continue speaking, he tapped his feet against the cold stone floor. "If I have to spend all that I have to make you as happy as you've made me, I will."

"Look at what you've given me." She turned to face him before looking down at her belly. "Next to being your wife, nothing could ever give me more joy than being the mother of your children."

He leaned and kissed the mounds of her full breasts. "You said children. That gives me hope that you're willing to go at least one more round."

The jetted bathtub in the center of the room sounded like water flowing over a peaceful brook.

"Sorry I missed the opportunity to sit in warm, bubbly water with you. It's probably a little cool by now." She inhaled. "The scent is divine." Tranquil aromatherapy filled the room. "Is that smell from the candles or from something in the water?"

She pointed at the white candles on the counter and on a table on the side of the room.

"Both. I had a Feng shui professional come in to make sure I was vibing with the right energy to create a harmonious space." He patted her bottom. "Enough talking. This time is about you. Change into your bikini and I'll help you get into the tub. It can maintain the water at a set temperature. Call me when you're ready to get out." He closed the curtains while she undressed.

Carly wasted no time tossing her heels aside, unbuttoning her shirt, and slipping out of her skirt while Mace leaned against the counter. She shimmied her hips and completely disrobed before going to the bench.

"You're such a teaser," he joked.

"Do you like it?" She looked over her shoulder before turning to face him, a classic, brown-skinned Madonna with child.

"Damn, girl." He crossed his leg over the other and placed his hands in his lap to hide his growing excitement.

She covered her mouth with her hands and giggled.

"You know I'm enjoying the show," he admitted before moaning with delight. "I don't want to sound like a cave man, but there is something primal, sensuous, and enticing seeing my woman barefoot and pregnant." He growled, pretending to be a lion. "Look at my seed growing inside you." He let out a breath to release his growing sexual tension.

"Help me?" She turned to let him tie the strings of her bikini top after she'd slipped on the black-laced bottom.

"Are you ready?" He drew back the curtains, the starry sky in its glory revealed. "I wasn't sure, but I thought someone in one of the other condos had a telescope pretending to look at the sky, but the lens was focused on you. Until I have a chance to have my security check it out, I recommend that you wear a bathing suit."

"Got it." She took his hand as he helped her in the bathtub.

"Take as much time as you like," he reminded her.

"Don't leave." She batted her eyelashes before sinking down into the water. "I don't want to be alone."

She rested her head against the back of the smooth porcelain top, soaking in deliciously warm water circulating with essential oils.

"This is heaven." She closed her eyes. "I smell…" She took another whiff. "Eucalyptus, lavender, and tea tree oils."

"You're correct." He walked to a chair and sat, observing Carly as she kept her eyes closed for a few minutes and slipped deeper into the water, succumbing to a deep state of relaxation. Mace got up and took off his shirt and pants, revealing his tear-away cotton shorts made of soft fabric with sides that were easy to unfasten in seconds.

"Babe, you're awake?"

She didn't respond. He climbed in, moving her relaxed body forward as she slept, before sinking deeper into the water. He supported her head against his chest.

"You're so beautiful." He placed his fingers in her hair and massaged her scalp in a tender circular motion.

She yawned and opened her eyes. "That felt good."

He turned on the micro-mister on the top of the bowl. A cloud of tiny water droplets pushed out of the machine, hydrating her hair as he stimulated her scalp. Comfortable that her body was braced against his and his legs were securely on both sides of her body, he was free to use his hands to undo her bikini top. After he slowed the speed of the water, the silken material floated on the water.

He took the top off a jar containing a substance that looked like soft, yellow butter. Covering his fingers with it, he pressed the cream along the top of her breast and rubbed it around the fullness of her breast then downward, traveling the length of her body.

"Oh my gosh." She pushed back against him and let out a breath. "What did I do to deserve you?"

"You love me." He took out another portion of the cream, covering his fingers. "Keep still or I won't be able to control myself. I want to make this all about you."

She didn't listen and his length, hardened like a steel rod, grew as she wiggled her bottom against him. He reached for the remote, watching the curtains close automatically before he tore off her bottom and slipped out of his shorts. Their privacy ensured, he rubbed the cream against her belly, moving slowly down to the triangle between her legs. She placed her hands on the tops of his thighs before letting out a deep, satisfied sound as he teased her tender nub, igniting her fires.

"You've always known how to turn me on."

"Your pleasure is my delight." He took the bottom of her earlobe into his mouth and sucked on it before he whispered, "I love you so much."

"I love you too." She moaned her pleasure and arched her back. Leaning her head against his chest, she surrendered to the ecstasy of his touch.

Steam curled up from the tub, wrapping the room in a soft, sultry haze. Carly's head leaned back against Mace's chest, her breath catching as his hands roamed her body, their movements slow, deliberate, full of intent. The water lapped gently at her skin, mimicking the rhythm of their bodies, but the heat between them was more intense than anything around them.

"You're so good to me," she whispered, her voice breaking as she arched into him, her hips swaying under his touch.

His fingers traced along her waist, guiding her movements, his strong arms pulling her closer until no space was left between them. She let out a soft moan, surrendering to the sensation, the world outside forgotten. Here, it was just him, just them.

Mace's heartbeat pounded against her back, each thump syncing with the slow roll of her hips as she rode the waves of her growing desire. Her excitement was electric, contagious, as he felt himself losing control, willingly swept up in the feverish pace she set. His hands slid down to her hips, gripping them as he moved in rhythm with her, the feeling of her body driving him deeper into their shared passion.

Carly's movements quickened, and he followed her lead, each thrust building toward a crescendo. Her breaths turned to gasps, and she shuddered against him, her release shaking her entire frame. He stilled for a moment, savoring the sounds of her pleasure before he slipped inside her, slowly, deliberately, letting her feel every inch.

This moment was hers. He reminded himself of that. This was about Carly—her body, her pleasure, her love. Mace was just the vessel, a man consumed by her, devoted to her. His muscles tightened, every stroke deeper, more insistent, until they were both trembling on the edge of oblivion.

His hands found her breasts, cupping them as he teased her nipples, drawing a breathless cry from her lips.

"Harder," she demanded, her voice full of hunger.

He didn't hesitate. His heart thundered as he responded, tightening his grip, driving into her with a fierceness that matched her desire. Carly threw her head back, gasping as the sensation overtook her. Every movement, every touch, ignited something deeper between them—a raw, primal connection that left him utterly undone.

"Faster," she commanded, her voice firm yet breathless.

Mace gave in completely, his need for control dissolving under the heat of her power. She had taken over, and he willingly followed her, lost in the rhythm of their bodies and the rush of their love.

He felt himself spiraling, no longer able to hold back. His release came fast, filling her with a warmth that matched the fire between them. The world outside their luxury spa faded, leaving only the pulse of their shared moment, their bodies entwined, moving as one. Mace's breaths came in shallow, ragged gasps as his hands still cradled her as if she might slip away.

But she wouldn't. She was his Carly. His and his alone. As she lay against him, her breathing slowing, her heart still racing, he closed his eyes and pressed a kiss to her damp shoulder. Anyone who dared to hurt her, to touch what was his, would answer to him. That was a certainty, a vow he would never break.

For now though, it was just them, wrapped in the warmth of the water, the love they shared flowing between them like an unbreakable bond. The quiet peace of their home wrapped around them, and Mace held her tighter, grateful for the woman who had captured his heart and for the life they were building together.

Chapter Eight

"WHY didn't you wake me?" Carly walked into the dining room, rubbing her eyes and dressed in a blue crop top that draped her belly and matching pants.

Rays of sun flooded the room painted in neutral tones with natural light. The round table was dressed in a starched linen tablecloth with crystal glasses containing water, orange juice, and tea. Pastries had been placed on fine China plates around a floral centerpiece.

"You needed the rest." Mace looked up from his tablet in front of him on the table. Dressed for the day in casual attire, he wore a collared white shirt and blue slacks. "You didn't move while I was getting dressed. You were naked and sprawled across the bed, a little too much temptation for me." He raised the corner of his mouth and wiggled his eyebrows.

"I like being a temptress when it comes to you." She crossed the room, walking toward him seated at the table. "Good morning." She leaned down with the intent to kiss him, but he pulled her onto his lap.

"You know how much I love looking at your belly." He looked at her with lidded eyes that didn't hide his lust. "I may have to find a robe for you to help me keep my hands off you while you eat."

"Who's asking you to keep your hands to yourself?" She placed her hands around his neck and gave him a kiss on the lips.

"You need to eat." He pointed at the food. "Marlena will kill me if she comes back and sees that you didn't touch your meal after I asked her to come here earlier to cook breakfast for us."

"You asked Marlena to come back to work without asking me first?" She pinched her lips together and rose from his lap. "I guess what I said yesterday still holds true. We need to talk."

She took a seat next to him.

"Tell Marlena I said thank you." She raised the dome covering her plate and looked at the meal containing waffles, egg whites, and an assortment of meats. "There's no way I can eat all of this."

"I know you wanted time to get used to living in the condo." He cut his sausage and placed a bite in his mouth. "It's been over three months since you moved in. Marlena has been my home manager for years. I agreed with you that she could use some time off, but she's itching to return full-time. We can talk about the date of her full return." He placed his fork alongside his plate. "In two weeks? What do you think?"

"I think we're not discussing things." Carly placed her fork on the side of her plate. "You decide and I'm expected to go along with your decisions."

He wiped his mouth with his napkin. "If that's how you see things, we need to talk."

"I like Marlena, but we already have a full house." She spoke in a slow, deliberate manner. "You're moving your office here, and there's always someone from your exec team around. It's either Andrew, Bernie, Chance, or all of the above."

"Don't forget my brother, Evan." He smirked.

"I'm being serious." A pinched expression crossed her face. "Sometimes they're here when you're not. I don't know if there's a strange man in the house with me or if he's one of your employees. Do you want them to see me naked?"

"That's a hard damn no," he said without thinking about it and ran his fingers through his hair. "I see your point. I'm asking for your patience as I try to work things out." He rubbed the back of his neck.

"I haven't moved the entire Charleston operation here. I just added a conference room so that I can be available after the baby comes."

"Understood, and that's not the only reason why I thought we needed to clear the air." She looked at him tightening his shoulders and sitting upright. Carly placed a hand over his and squeezed it. "I'm not accusing you of anything or finding fault with your decisions. I just think we need to know where each other stand."

"I'd feel better if you eat while we talk." He softened his expression.

"I can do that." She smiled now that the ice was broken, allowing them time to talk about things. She picked up her fork and placed a piece of her waffle in her mouth. "After yesterday's attack, I feel strongly that you need to let me know what's going on with Nala's suit against your company. I'm not saying she had anything to do with it, but the *coincidences* are adding up. She was at the restaurant, in my class, and at the shop yesterday."

"I haven't said anything because her suit is baseless. Both Evan and Ariel think so. She was the one who missed the final payment of her bill to rent the space at the time that was agreed to in a written contract. Yes, my company paid the full amount, in cash, to rent the space for our reception, but I didn't steal anything from her. It was available."

"Okay." She nodded. "That's good to know. I don't want vengeance to fuel something that could end up hurting people I care about, like Yara. I need to check on her. I'll call her in a little bit on Aunt Nora's house phone." *Thud.* She lowered her palm on the table, recalling yesterday's trauma. "We were attacked, I'm worried about her, and neither of us have cell phones."

"Don't worry," he reassured Carly. "She called about an hour ago from Aunt Nora's. She's doing fine. I told her I would replace her cell phone."

"I'm glad she's okay, but that's the other thing. Why are you replacing her phone?"

"Why would you even ask that?" He furrowed his brow. "Why not?"

"Why did you buy Yara a car and now a cell phone?" She sat back in her chair, awaiting his answer.

"You've assumed I bought Yara a car when I didn't." He crossed his hands on the table. "I did a favor for a friend whose family owns a Lexus dealership. He told me to pick any car I wanted. You"—he emphasized, pointing at her—"told me Yara needed a car, and she liked the Lexus brand. Since neither one of us needed a car, I had my friend deliver it to her."

"Did you have time to discuss it with me *before* you gave it to her?" She pursed her lips.

"Of course I had time, but why spoil the surprise? The look on both of your faces was priceless."

She sighed. "Don't get me wrong, I appreciate your generosity, but I would prefer that you pay Yara and Ariel for consultation services they are providing the company instead of getting them expensive gifts." She placed her elbow on the table and cupped her chin.

"They won't take the money, babe." He took her hand. "I understand that you don't want our money to be an issue between you and your girls. I'm not trying to buy your friends."

"Thank you." She blew out a breath. "Been there, done that." She looked away, memories of a shared past flashing through her mind.

"I remember that falling out between you and your friend at the time, Sharon Sumter, on Folly Beach." He rolled his eyes. "That was some drama."

"Are you telling me you remember what happened over ten years ago?" Her jaw slackened.

"How could I forget?" He chuckled. "On one side there was team Carly—well, at the time, you were team Caroline—and on the other there was team Sharon."

"What did you hear about it?' She placed her elbows on the table and gave him her full attention.

"You and those girls were *Love and Hip-Hop Miami* before the show was created." He smiled.

"Stop it," she remarked and threw her napkin at him.

"As I understand it," he said, looking around as if he was about to tell a secret that lurking ears shouldn't hear, "you and some of the other cheerleaders gave money so that Sharon and another girl on the squad could afford to pay their share for the beach house on Folly Beach for spring break. You were all staying at the house next to my grandparents' house. They allowed me and a few of my football buddies to stay there for that week."

"Continue." She smiled. "I've got to hear this."

"Sharon brought a second girl without telling you and the other cheerleaders."

"Her name was Sabrina," Carly added.

"Right… that's right, and you all called her Breena." He pointed his index finger then rested it upon his chin. "I digress. The house had five bedrooms, but Sharon ended up sleeping in your bed since there was no more room in the inn. Do I have it right so far?"

"Go on," she encouraged.

"I saw you outside on the porch, early in the morning before the blowup. That's the first time we watched the sun come up together. I remember it was a beautiful sunrise over the Atlantic Ocean."

"It was." She looked at him with dreamy eyes.

"Even though we've known each other most of our lives, I was seeing you as a woman for the first time. I loved what I saw." He pressed both hands over his heart. "I wanted to be your man."

"That's not what I recall." She wrinkled her nose as if the scent of her memories was still offensive. "Breena was throwing herself at you all week. I remember someone saying that she moved into your bedroom and you gave her money since, as you say, there was no room at the inn."

"I wasn't sharing my bedroom, that was just a rumor. I had already told your brother, John, that I wanted to be your man, but he got caught up in the rumor. He was my bro, and up until then, we were having a bromance." He laughed. "I thought he would be glad that the two of us were getting together. Instead, he told me that he would kick my ass if I made a move on you. At the time, I was risking my one hundred eighty pounds tussling with his two hundred ten pounds of mostly muscle. He called me a *man-hoe* and said that I should get my act together before even considering a date with you. John and I have been close since elementary school. He's always had my back, but when it came to you, he wasn't having it. He told me I didn't have the right to break your heart. He didn't care who I was, and he stormed off. The last time I saw him that day, he had his bag on his shoulder, and he told me he was leaving."

"He never shared that with me." She cocked her head. "I thought he heard that I'd had some heated words with Breena and Sharon, and that's why he acted the way he did."

"Why were you and Breena having words?" He leaned forward.

"They were words… over you." She looked at her fingers.

"I see. The story is still interesting after all these years." His eyes brightened.

She hesitated before continuing. "I told her she was making a fool of herself in front of everyone. Even a blind person could see she was trying to get your attention, and it wasn't wanted."

"Were you jealous? Tell the truth." He nudged her shoulder, egging her on.

"A little," she rushed to admit. "Sharon didn't like that I confronted her friend, and the other cheerleaders didn't like that Breena was there in the first place. It set off a war of words between all of us before John knocked on the door and told me we were leaving."

"After you left, it was more than a war of words. The guys from the team had to go over there to break up the catfight." He tried containing his humor, but moments later, he was bent over in laughter. He hit the table with his palm, his body shaking before he regained control. "I never saw so much hair pulling and faces getting slapped in my life." He motioned like a cat pouncing with its claws drawn.

His laughter was infectious, and before long, Carly was in tears from laughing with him. After they both calmed, she looked at him in silence for a few moments.

This man for so long had been the catalyst for so many emotions… happiness, anger, disappointment, and coming full circle back to joy.

"What?" He looked at her. "What are you thinking?"

"I know why Breena wanted you so badly." Her gaze reflected a truth, a way of looking at him that came from her soul. "You're beautiful, Mace."

"Huh?" He stopped smiling.

"When I look at you, I see your beauty, inside and out. It's easy for others to see how handsome you are. Your gorgeous brown eyes, your perfectly shaped lips, and your cute nose grab attention."

"Stop it." His cheeks darkened and he waved her off. "Are you trying to embarrass me?"

"I said we needed to talk, and it's a part of what I want to say to you. Thank you."

"For what exactly? I need to hear when I do things right because you know I'm going to need your forgiveness when I get it wrong."

"Thank you for taking care of me last night—the spa you created, your tenderness, making me feel safe again—and for letting me know that we still have a lot to laugh about despite the craziness Nala is trying to create."

"Come here." He motioned for her. "I could never do enough to show you how grateful I am that we're back together and that my child is also your child." He took her in his lap and lowered his head to kiss her belly.

"I hope the baby looks like you." She cradled his face in her hands.

"You want our girl to look like me?"

"I keep telling you that I don't know if we're having a girl." She touched her belly. "I looked like my father, and my mother used to tell me that when a girl looks like her father, she's blessed. So, boy or girl, I want it to look like you."

"Time will tell." He kissed her lips. "Are we finished talking?"

She nodded.

"Good, because I have something else to say that will require that you take your clothes off. Shall we go back to the bedroom?"

"Yes," she answered before turning her head toward the sound of the door opening.

"Boss, it's me. Andrew."

"I need to change some things." Mace placed Carly on her feet.

"I agree." She straightened her clothes. "See what he wants. I need to change my clothes."

CHAPTER NINE

MACE pulled into the driveway, his mind racing through the events of the last twenty-four hours. He cut the engine, his fingers tightening on the steering wheel as he took a deep breath, willing himself to stay calm. After leaving Carly to rest at the condo, he'd gone through a whirlwind of meetings, but now, as the silence of Aunt Nora's home loomed before him, the weight of his worry settled in. He grabbed the bouquet of flowers Andrew had picked up and walked to the door, every step filled with tension.

Before he could knock, Aunt Nora appeared, her expression unreadable. "Hello, Mason. You just missed Carly and Daniel. She dropped him at the airport and headed to her office to pick up some work."

Mace froze, his pulse quickening. *Carly went to the office? Alone? After what happened?* His jaw clenched. "Wait. You're telling me Carly was here?"

Aunt Nora raised an eyebrow. "Unless there's an echo around here, that's what I said." She waved him in. "Are you going to stand there, or do you want to come inside?"

He stepped over the threshold, his muscles tense. "I wasn't expecting her to leave the condo. I came to check on Yara." He glanced around the warm, inviting room, the family mementos lining the walls doing little to ease his rising anxiety. "She called earlier. I said I'd stop by here after my meetings."

As if summoned by his words, Yara emerged from the hallway, her face pale but composed. "Hi, Mace." She smiled weakly, accepting the bouquet of flowers he offered.

"I wanted to make sure you're all right," Mace said, his voice low. "Carly told me what happened yesterday."

"Thanks for the new phone," Yara said, her smile faltering. "Aunt Nora's been fussing over me, but I'm okay." Her phone buzzed, and her gaze shifted toward the bedroom. "Sorry, I've been expecting a call. I'll be right back." She hurried off, leaving Mace alone with Aunt Nora.

Aunt Nora studied him for a moment, her sharp eyes missing nothing. "You seem surprised Carly came by today." She motioned for him to sit. "Why? Is there something you're not telling me?"

Mace sat stiffly, his heart pounding. "It's just… I didn't think she'd be out and about so soon, not after what happened. The police believe it was a random attack, another of a string of thefts in the area, not a personal attack on her and Yara."

Aunt Nora leaned forward, her expression skeptical. "Random or not, I'm worried about Carly. She's running herself ragged with work, projects, and now this party, a masquerade ball. You need to slow her down before something worse happens."

"I've talked to her," Mace replied, anxiety creeping into his voice. "But maybe she'll listen if it comes from you."

Aunt Nora chuckled, shaking her head. "That girl's always been hard-headed. But if anyone can get through to her, it's you. Just make sure she knows she's pushing herself too far."

Before Mace could respond, Yara reappeared. "That was Preston," she said, her voice steady, though her eyes betrayed a sense of unease. "He called to check on me after hearing about the attack."

"I'll leave you two to talk," Aunt Nora said before walking toward the kitchen.

Mace's brow furrowed. "Preston? Nala's ex?"

"Yeah. Preston Nigel Smith has a shop, The Nautical Press, near the Clarke's Bajan Imports Store. It's a bookstore and gift shop. He heard about what happened from customers." Yara sat down next to

Mace, her fingers nervously tapping on her phone. "He warned us to be careful. Carly and I visited the Clarke's Bajan Imports Store before the attack, and now I'm not sure it was such a good idea."

Mace leaned forward, his voice dropping. "Why? What's going on, Yara?"

She hesitated before pulling out her phone. "Carly noticed some strange markings on the back of the ceramics we looked at. I took pictures, but they've been wiped from my phone. Whoever did it, they're good. The data's gone from the cloud too."

Mace's jaw tightened. "If there's a connection, it's less likely that this was a random attack. Call my tech team. They'll help you retrieve whatever's left." He paused, the weight of the situation pressing down on him. "Carly's been pushing me to put you and Ariel on the payroll. She wants clear lines between my business and our friendship. We talked about it, and I understand her concerns."

"All right, I may need some help from your associates with this *project*," she relented. "I'll be out of town on another matter starting tomorrow morning. I'm not sure when I can come back, but I should be back before the masquerade ball."

"Expect a call from my company's HR soon," Mace told her.

Yara nodded, though her mind was clearly elsewhere. "Mace... I've been digging into Preston's background. He's no ordinary guy. Former Naval intelligence. He's got serious security protocols in place. It's taking longer than usual to get any solid intel. For a regular private citizen, Preston has set up a lot of firewalls on his data. I usually get information on most people in minutes. It took hours to get what I was able to discover."

Mace's gaze darkened as he leaned back, hands behind his neck. "How much does Carly know?"

"Everything," Yara said. "She's suspicious of him too."

Mace stood abruptly, the tension in his body coiled tight. "The invitations for the masquerade ball have already gone out. If Preston calls again, encourage him to come."

Yara blinked, looking surprised. “You think he’s involved in all this?”

“I’m not sure,” Mace admitted, glancing at the peaceful greenery surrounding Aunt Nora’s porch. The calm felt like a lie masking the danger lurking beneath the surface. “But I’m not taking any chances.”

Yara rose to her feet, determination darting in her eyes. “I’ll handle it. I’ll also keep digging into Nala’s background. Something about all of this doesn’t sit right with me.”

“Good,” Mace said, resting a hand on her shoulder. “I need to get home. Aunt Nora was right. Carly’s pushing herself too hard.”

Yara smirked, raising a finger. “Just remember, it wasn’t me who spilled the beans about her errands. Aunt Nora did. I’m not the snitch here.”

Mace chuckled, but the weight of everything still hung heavily in the air. “Help me convince Carly to accept a security detail. I need to do all I can to keep her safe.”

Yara nodded, her expression hardening. “Deal. And Mace? Be careful. I’m starting to think this whole thing is a lot more complicated than it seems.”

Mace gave her a grim smile, his concern for Carly mounting. “So am I.” He turned to leave. “One more thing, Yara. I know you and Chance Baker may have a thing going on. I’ve known him for a long time. He’s a beast in business, but those skills don’t make for a good boyfriend.”

“Who said I was looking for a boyfriend?” She rolled her eyes.

“As long as you know what you’re getting into.” He placed his hands in his pocket and walked to his car.

“I can take care of myself,” she said in a loud voice. “I’ve never known all of what I was getting myself into, but it has never stopped me from diving in headfirst,” she muttered and went back inside.

Mace looked at her walk into the house. He sensed a dark cloud of uncertainty hanging over all of them.

***

"Thanks for meeting with me." Carly extended her hand to the attractive gentleman in designer casual wear with a bright smile exposing his pearly white teeth. He had personally called to invite her to a tour of Clarke's Bajan Imports.

"I'm Simeon Clarke." He shook her hand. "I appreciate your interest in my business. My assistant overheard you talking to my sister, Nala. You asked to speak to the manager or owner. That would be me." He pointed at himself and laughed.

Carly joined in, smiling at him but sensing that there may have been more to his amusement. *But what?*

"How can I help you?" He leaned closer. "My parents started this business. Did Nala tell you our mother was an accomplished artist before she took ill? She loved Bajan art and mastered the craft during her years living in Barbados."

She shook her head. "I didn't know that, but what I was interested in were the unusual markings on some of the pieces." She picked up a ceramic plate and turned it around. "Curious?"

She wrinkled her brow. The plate didn't have the markings she'd noticed the day before. Instead, it had the signature of an artist she had met during her honeymoon on the island.

"I have several of this artist's pieces."

"I think you're referring to the basketweave pattern my mother and grandmother used to distinguish their pieces." He took another piece off the shelf. "Are you referring to this marking?"

Carly took the plate from him, and on the back of it was the marking with horizontal and vertical interlocking lines. "This is the mark. I don't recall seeing it on any of the pieces during my tour of the island."

"We have exclusive rights to our family's designs," he explained. "You wouldn't have seen it in the island shops. We also sell designs created by people from the island of Barbados. That's why we call it imports of Bajan origin. The pieces are mass-produced in factories where we employ many people."

"I see." Carly walked around the shop with Simeon following behind her.

"Nala must not have shared with you that we come from a family of means. My father was a lawyer, and reportedly, we're distant relatives of George Carter, the first African American judge born in Canada. His parents migrated from Barbados."

"I didn't know that." She took a small pad out of her bag and wrote down the name. "I'll have to do a little research on him. Thanks for sharing."

"I'll be happy to share what I know about my paternal side of the family. Do you have more questions? If not, I have some questions for you."

Carly turned to give him her attention. "What's on your mind?"

"Well, for one, I wondered if your husband was planning on purchasing property in this area? You know they say when Mason Moore moves, the world shudders."

"I don't think I've ever heard that before." She looked into Simeon's eyes, realizing that his statement about Mace wasn't a compliment. "I'm not closely involved in his business dealings."

"Surely you can't be serious." He walked alongside her. "Behind every successful man is often the true power behind the throne."

"Why are you concerned about his business dealings?" She stopped, causing him to almost bump into her.

"The parking around here is already a problem. You can always tell when he and his business associates are around. There's the usual entourage of black vehicles filled with his execs and security detail. The local authorities often show up too. Who wouldn't want to know his next move?"

"Mace and I have chosen different career paths." She paused, not wanting to air thoughts she hadn't completely processed. "Let's say that my path is quieter and less glamorous."

"Interesting." He lifted his chin. "I was prepared for a meeting with a woman who had her own personal driver and group of security guys."

"Why?" She pursed her lips. "We haven't been married that long. Thanks to his ex-wife, Jamillah, an international supermodel, most of the pictures on social media are of her and not me."

"You're comfortable with that?" He raised an eyebrow. "Surely a man with the money he's reported to have also has made his share of enemies. I heard that you and your friend were attacked. I wouldn't allow something like that to happen again if you were my wife. That's all I'm saying."

"Let's say that the things that make me comfortable or uncomfortable are my business." She watched while his expression darkened. "I thank you for the invitation and your personal attention."

"The pleasure was all mine." He moved to the side.

"Goodbye." Carly walked to the door and exited the shop. "I don't think he arranged this meeting to talk about cups and plates."

She walked a block away from the shop to get back to her car. After turning on the engine, she looked at the radio and snickered. The song "Smooth Criminal" played as she maneuvered from the curb and headed downtown.

Carly stepped out of the car, the late afternoon sun casting long shadows across the university campus. A light breeze brushed her face, the air cool despite the waning daylight. The thoughts of her encounter with Simeon Clarke lingered, but she pushed them aside. She glanced at the building, the familiar sight of her new office window making her stomach churn with both relief and dread. Her former office, sealed with police crime tape, stood across the hall as a silent reminder of everything that had happened.

"Where has the time gone?" she muttered as she slid her key into the door of her current office.

The hallway felt eerily empty, the typical hustle of faculty and students long gone, replaced by a stillness that made her feel exposed. She paused, her hand hesitating on the knob. The muffled sounds of distant footsteps made her chest tighten, but she forced herself inside.

The door clicked shut behind her, and she exhaled sharply, trying to shake the feeling of being watched. She dropped her bag on the desk and stared at the empty chair across from her. She should be at home, but home didn't feel like the sanctuary it had been before Mace moved some of his business operations into the condo. She was no longer expecting the spontaneous moments of connection, those small, precious times when they could just *be* alone together. The sunrise walks on the beach. The quiet dinners. Things had changed since they'd left Barbados. Her fingers traced the edge of her desk as she powered on her computer.

She sat down, shifting uncomfortably. Her growing pregnancy made it harder to settle in. She had changed her hours to get more rest, but the suspicious death of an employee last seen in her office and the recent attack had thrown everything off kilter. Her appointments, canceled because of Mace's concerns, and her work had been left undone. She sighed, scrolling through the mountain of unread emails.

Outside her office came muffled sounds. Carly's heart skipped a beat when she heard keys clanging against her door. The noise pierced the quiet, making her pulse quicken. "Who would be here this late?" Her fingers froze above the keyboard as her doorknob turned. She stared at it, tension building in her limbs, fear crawling up her spine. The voice in her head, Simeon's voice, echoed, "I was prepared for a meeting with a woman who had her own personal driver and group of security guys."

Her breath came faster, her muscles tight with adrenaline. *Stay calm*. She reached into her desk drawer, her fingers wrapping around the metal letter opener. The blade's cool weight in her hand offered little comfort.

The door opened slowly, and her grip tightened. But it wasn't a threat. The familiar figure of the security guard stood there, his expression neutral.

"Professor," he greeted, "I wasn't expecting anyone to be here this late. You all right?"

Carly let out a shaky breath, trying to steady her voice. "I'm fine. Just needed to grab a few things."

He gave her a nod, his eyes scanning the room. "You need an escort to your car?"

She forced a smile. "No, I'll be fine. I won't be here much longer."

He left, closing the door softly, but the sense of unease remained. Moments later, the sound of footsteps echoed in the hallway again, this time sharper, quicker. Heels. Carly's heart skipped again, her body instinctively tensing.

Then another figure appeared in Carly's office doorway. Nala.

Carly stiffened. The sight of her brought an unwelcome twist in her gut. Nala, in her casual jeans and T-shirt, was nothing like the polished, poised version Carly usually saw. She carried thick construction gloves and goggles, looking more like she belonged at a renovation site than in Carly's office.

"This must be my lucky day," Nala said, her tone light, but Carly wasn't fooled. Lucky for who? Nala waved with her free hand. "Hi, Professor. Since I'm not enrolled full-time, can I just call you Carly?"

Carly bit back a sigh, tilting her head instead. "All my students call me Dr. Moore or Professor Carly. Take your pick."

Nala raised an eyebrow. "I'm not officially your student though." She shifted into a seat, fidgeting with her gloves. "I'm auditing through the outreach program. I already have a degree."

Carly sat up straighter, folding her hands neatly on her desk. "Then what brings you here? If this is about tomorrow's project, Mr. Stone will handle that."

But Nala leaned forward, her eyes narrowing. "I need to know… why did you choose the last weekend in March for your wedding reception?"

Carly blinked, taken aback. "What?" *This was about her wedding reception? Again.* "I don't think we should be having this conversation. Especially considering you're suing my husband."

Nala's face tightened. Her hands clenched the gloves. "My brother, Simeon… he's been pressuring me to drop the suit. But I just—" Her voice wavered, and tears formed in her eyes. "I can't help feeling like everything fell apart for me that weekend."

Carly's eyes softened, but her walls stayed up. "What does any of this have to do with me?" She inhaled deeply, searching for patience. "Nala, you should've asked questions before involving lawyers." She pulled out her phone, scrolling through photos until she landed on one of her mother. She held it out for Nala to see. "This is why we chose that weekend. My mother, Mellie Jones Rivers, was born on March 29th. She passed three years ago, and I wanted her to be a part of the celebration."

Nala's eyes flicked to the photo. "She was beautiful," she murmured, before glancing back at Carly. "So… it had nothing to do with me?"

Carly's patience was thinning. "No. We didn't know you."

Nala's expression hardened. "Maybe not, but Jamillah did. She warned me about Mason. Said he only cares about his business deals. You'll find out he's just using you."

Carly remained silent, her pulse steadying as she observed cracks in Nala's cool veneer. *This woman is unraveling.*

The sound of footsteps returned—this time the security guard again. "You still here, Professor?"

Carly smiled, standing slowly. "Yes, but not for long. Please escort Ms. Clarke to her car." Her tone left no room for debate.

Nala gathered her things, shooting Carly one last, unreadable glance. "Tell Mason thanks for the party invite."

When she walked out, the guard followed, casting Carly a knowing look as he closed the door.

Carly sighed heavily, the weight of everything pressing down on her. "The road to hell really is paved with good intentions." She gathered her papers, her mind racing with everything yet to come.

Chapter Ten

MACE woke early, the dark clouds overhead mirroring his thoughts. His home office, usually a sanctuary, felt confined as the rain fell. Carly emerged hours later, her presence warming the space. She sat across from him, her frustration evident even before she spoke.

"Did you eat breakfast?" Mace asked, his lips brushing hers in a soft kiss before he joined her in the adjacent chair.

"I did." Carly frowned, glancing out the window. "I can't believe it's been dry all week, and now, today of all days, it rains." Her voice tightened as she crossed her legs, her black jeans and long-sleeved shirt emphasizing her focus on the renovation project looming over her.

"The rain should stop by noon," Mace reassured, placing a hand on her knee. "Sam's team is already on-site, starting what they can before the volunteers arrive."

She nodded, her fingers brushing her lips in thought. "Thank you. You and Sam have been godsends. I couldn't have done it without you."

She blew him a playful kiss, but Mace's expression shifted, his face clouding over like the sky outside.

Her brow furrowed. "What's wrong?"

"One of my investigators got word from a contact at the police station," Mace said, voice low. "They've identified the guy who attacked you."

Carly's jaw clenched. "Have they caught him?"

"Not yet," Mace said, his stubble catching the dim light as he rubbed his cheek. "He's the brother of the delivery guy who brought you lunch that day. We've got footage from the cameras at the school and on the street where the sandwich shop is located. It's good they were installed, despite Clarke's objections about street cameras near his business."

Her shoulders sagged. "Mr. Simeon Clarke, of course." She sighed heavily. "If it seems too coincidental, it probably isn't."

Mace's jaw tightened. "Exactly. We're connecting the dots."

Carly leaned forward, her voice sharp. "I appreciate you telling me, but you know I've dealt with men hiding things before. I learned to sharpen my sword and handle my dragons. I can fight tough battles."

Mace's eyes darkened as he met her gaze. "I know you can fight, but as my wife, you shouldn't have to. I've got your back." His voice held a promise, one he seemed determined to keep.

She moved onto his lap, watching him struggle to contain his emotions. "I've got yours too," she whispered, her hand resting over his heart.

Mace swallowed hard, his arms tightening around her. "You never turned anyone against me, not even after we broke up years ago. You had my back when I didn't deserve it."

"I never saw you as the bad guy," she murmured, leaning her head on his shoulder. "I just thought we weren't meant to be."

Mace glanced down, his hand splaying across her belly. "I'm glad you were wrong."

As their conversation wound down, Carly stood and walked toward the window, her posture betraying the emotions simmering beneath the surface. "The rain's letting up," she said, a hopeful note in her voice.

Mace rose, his expression more guarded now. "Try to keep your distance from Nala at the event. I've got people handling her."

Carly turned to him, her eyes narrowing. "That's easier said than done. She's been stirring up media attention, and we need that. But don't worry, I won't meet with her alone."

Mace nodded, unease lingering in the air between them as they parted ways for a day filled with obligations.

***

Later that afternoon, Mace sat in Evan's office, the air thick with tension. His brother, as sharp as ever, handed him documents to review, but Mace's thoughts were elsewhere.

"You're paying me the big bucks to tell it like it is," Evan said, sitting behind his desk. "You haven't done anything wrong, but engaging with someone like Nala? Not worth the risk."

Mace scowled. "I didn't start this fight, but I'm sure as hell not walking away from it."

Evan leaned back in his chair, holding up a stack of papers with a grim expression. "Look, Mace, Ms. Clarke could've taken this fight straight to the court of public opinion. It's a nightmare for any multinational, especially when you're cast as Goliath. But here's the reality—none of this has hurt your business." He flipped through the pages. "The press isn't biting. No one's feeling the heat. Hell, Nala's posts about the case barely gained traction. Her engagement is dipping."

Mace raised a brow, skeptical. "Is that right?"

Evan nodded, giving a thumbs-up. "Facts. Your stock prices are climbing, even while this whole mess unfolds. Whatever she's trying, it's not affecting your bottom line."

"So, I'm still on that Fortune 500 list?" Mace smirked, leaning back in his chair with a hint of arrogance.

"You're not just on it, you've moved up." Evan tossed the papers onto the desk with a sense of finality. "But listen, her lawyers reached out with a proposal. They'll drop the case if, as a gesture of goodwill, you and Carly give Nala exclusive rights to the first pictures of the baby for her blog. She's pitching it as some 'forgive and move on' PR stunt."

Mace stood abruptly, his disbelief shifting into sharp laughter. "Forgive me and Carly? What in the world does she have to forgive us for?" His laughter grew darker as he wiped a tear from his eye, unable to contain his outrage. "So, what you're telling me is she wants photos of our child as some kind of peace offering? No. Absolutely not."

"Then how about offering a financial settlement?" Evan suggested, keeping his tone even. "Maybe reimburse her for the deposit she lost on that reception hall. I know you want this gone."

Mace shot him a steely look, but Evan raised his hands, cutting off the retort he knew was coming. "Hear me out. I'm more concerned about your personal investigation into Nala, Preston, and her brother, Simeon. That man has a reputation, Mace. The attack on Carly, it happened right after you started eyeing a property he wanted. You've already moved on to a different deal. Maybe now is the time to let this go."

Mace stopped pacing, his hands gripping the edge of the desk. His voice dropped, simmering with barely controlled rage. "Someone attacked my wife."

Evan stood firm. "And you can't prove any of them were involved."

The unease between them thickened, two brothers locked in a silent battle of wills, their brown eyes—so alike in intensity—narrowed in a quiet showdown. The intercom buzzed, breaking the standoff.

"Your next appointment is here, Mr. Moore," Evan's assistant announced.

"Give me five minutes," Evan responded before looking up at Mace. "I have a pro bono case I agreed to take."

Mace's jaw clenched, his finger pressing the button as he turned his gaze back to Evan. "He won't need five minutes."

Evan sighed, finally relenting. "Let's talk more about this when you've cooled off." He walked around the desk, giving Mace's shoulder a brotherly pat before grabbing his jacket.

As they headed toward the door, Evan spoke, his voice softer. "Look, I get it. Family is everything. I'd do anything for Kate and my kids. But you and me? We have different ways of handling threats. I handle things in the courtroom; you're more comfortable handling them in the streets. But you don't have to turn to the streets, Mace. Let me look into this matter further to get us ready for a court battle, if necessary."

Mace glanced at him, his expression unyielding. "I don't need to get ready, Evan. I stay ready. Legal or not, men have come after me before. I know how to handle my business."

Evan's hand paused on the door. "That's exactly what concerns me," he said as he opened it.

Mace stepped out, but his path was blocked by a woman standing in the waiting area. Her presence was striking. Thick curls framed her face like a crown, and her swollen belly made her look almost regal, despite the sadness that lingered behind her warm eyes.

"Are you Mason Moore?" she asked, her voice soft but determined as she pointed at him, her lips slightly parted in surprise.

Mace nodded, used to the attention his public profile brought.

"Congratulations," she said, extending her hand. "I saw the pictures of you and your wife in the newspaper's society section. You two looked so happy, and she's just… beautiful. I could see the love between you, clear as day, and I heard you're expecting a baby. That's wonderful."

Evan stepped forward, clearly eager to wrap this up. "Ma'am, we really need to—"

Mace waved him off. "It's fine." He turned his attention back to her. "What's your name?"

"Emily Bradley. Well, Emily Anne, if you ask my friends." She smiled shyly, as if the name meant something deeper to her.

"Nice to meet you, Emily Anne." Mace reached into his jacket and handed her a business card. "My wife and I are very active in the community. Let us know if you ever need anything."

"Thank you," Emily said, clutching the card as if it was a lifeline before tucking it into her bag.

Evan raised a brow at Mace, silently reminding him of their earlier conversation. “Don’t forget what we talked about, brother. Watch your exposure.”

Mace smiled faintly, waving goodbye. “I’ve got you watching my back, right? No need to worry.”

With a final glance at Emily, Mace walked out, leaving Evan to handle the rest.

Chapter Eleven

Thud. Bam. Bam.

Hammers hitting metal nails and driving them into wood, the whirling of electric saws, and the footsteps of workers in steel-toe shoes scurrying around filled the home under renovation.

"I'm glad the rain finally stopped," Carly said as she cupped her hands around her mouth. Her attempts were futile. The noise on the busy construction site drowned out her voice.

"I can't hear you," Ariel yelled back. Carly motioned for her to join her outside.

"I said I'm glad the rain stopped," she repeated in a normal volume. "I'm so glad you could come."

"I wasn't sure if I was going make it. The flight from Washington, DC, was delayed because of the weather. Yara didn't think she would be back in time."

Both were dressed in hard hats, gloves, safety goggles, and closed-toe shoes. Ariel pointed at the group of women in the front of the house dressed differently from the rest of the volunteers. Nala stood with the group of women in full makeup.

"Who are they with the silver hats and matching gloves?" Ariel asked. "I didn't know you recruited the fashion squad for this project."

Ariel and Carly leaned closer to each other and smiled.

"Nala ordered the safety suits for her *girls.*" Carly raised an eyebrow. "They have designer belts around their waists and silver buckles on their suits."

"Why?" Ariel shook her head.

Carly shrugged.

"Listen, there are too many people in the building," Sam Stone, safety manager on the project, yelled out. "This is a construction site, not a photo shoot."

"I think they're getting on his last nerve." Ariel peered through the door.

"Let's go back inside. Sam has been a godsend. I don't want him so frustrated that he refuses to work on other projects in the future."

They walked back inside and stood beside Sam speaking to Nala.

"Okay, guys." Nala motioned to her team of photographers. "That's enough shots. Pack up and I'll review them later today." She clapped her hands.

All the volunteers stopped speaking in response to Nala claiming their attention. Sam took advantage of the lull in activity to make his announcement.

"Listen up, everybody." He waited as the participants gathered around him. "I only have ten people certified to use the compressed air nail guns, according to OSHA standards. These are the people who came to the safety training and passed the verification. Please, everyone, if your name isn't on the list, use the regular hammers and saws only."

Sam and his crew of professionals who worked on projects for Mace's company had come in the morning and finished most of the work on the inside prior to the arrival of the volunteers. There was still painting, shelving, and finishing decorative touches that could be completed by volunteers who had no prior experience.

Those who had completed the training knew not to carry the nail gun by the handle or walk around with their finger on the trigger.

"I think I'll work with the crew on the shelving for one of the reading nooks," Ariel told Carly.

"The top shelf is a bit high for you." Sam added. "Let me get a ladder and I'll put in the taller shelves, then you can complete the rest."

Ariel and Sam left Carly standing in the center of the room. She had no specific assignments, which allowed her to troubleshoot. She looked out of the corner of her eye and saw Nala grabbing the nail gun from one of the *girls* who was certified in its use. Nala was not.

Before Carly could intervene, *Pow*! The gun unexpectedly fired, followed by another loud blast. *Pow. Pow*!

Folks scrambled away from the nails traveling at high speed, hissing as they flew across the room. Carly broke out in a sweat and fogged her glasses. Fear clawed at her throat, stopping her from screaming. Her vision blurred from the trail of nails speeding past her.

She thought she heard Mace yelling, "Look out."

One of the nails ricocheted off the metal refrigerator that was to be placed in the kitchen and tattered the uniform of one of the volunteers. His material became blood-stained before the nail imbedded itself in the wall behind him.

Sam pushed Ariel out of the way, but the second nail caught Ariel's oversized safety jacket and anchored her to the wall like a stake. Sam helped her out of her jacket, freeing her shoulder.

"Are you all right?" He examined her shoulder for signs of injury.

"I'm all right." Ariel placed a hand over her chest. "Just a little shaken up."

"Everybody put your weapons… I mean work tools down." Mace stormed into the room and turned his attention to Nala.

"It was an accident." She lowered the nail gun and slowly placed it on the floor.

Carly came forward and stood between Mace and Nala. "Let me handle this please." She felt his fury as he blew deep breaths into the air. "Calm down."

"I've already called 9-1-1." Carly's assistant at the university came forward. "They said to apply pressure to the wound. There's an ambulance on the way."

Sam had already gone to the injured volunteer and torn off his uniform. He examined the man's injured leg and applied pressure with gauze from one of the safety kits. "It's a flesh wound."

"Thank you, Sam." Carly raised her hands to reassure the rest of the group. "We only have a few tasks remaining. Will the group leaders for painting gather your group and head to the bedrooms while the rest of you follow the leaders to the kitchen to set up the new appliances? The last group, follow the leaders to place the decorative touches around the house."

Everyone left Nala in the room with Mace, Carly, Sam, and Ariel.

"Nala, can you join me in the family room?" Carly asked.

She nodded and followed Carly—with Ariel following them after receiving a nonverbal sign from Mace.

"Thank you for your assistance, but I think you should leave. You didn't come to any of the safety meetings, and your actions led to the injury of another person."

Nala looked at the floor. "I'm sorry. It was an accident."

"I still need you to leave," Carly insisted.

"All right, but I raised thousands of dollars for this project. The donors are expecting that I'll be at the masquerade party."

Carly closed her eyes, centering herself. Ariel placed a hand on her shoulder.

"Your invitation hasn't been rescinded at this point," Ariel said. Carly sensed her friend had shifted into lawyer mode. "We have your information if we need to contact you."

Nala turned and left the room.

"I don't want to speak badly of anyone, but that girl is a walking disaster," Carly opined.

Ariel tightened her lips and nodded.

Chapter Twelve

"ARE you sure you're up to coming to the masquerade party tonight?" Mace fastened the tie around his neck that coordinated with his custom black tuxedo.

"I'm almost dressed." Carly placed gold earrings in her ears. "Why would I back out now?"

Her stylist had picked accessories that coordinated with her tea-length dress with its fashionable high-waisted bodice adorned with a black butterfly bow and a flared asymmetrical green satin skirt that fell beautifully over her growing baby bump. Looking in the mirror one last time, she was happy with her look—which included strappy sensible heels. Her bump was becoming more noticeable as the months passed. Dressing in stilettos was out of the question.

"I'm asking because when Marlena was here cleaning up, she said you were sprawled out on the bed. She described you as sleeping like the dead. You hardly moved."

"I was tired, but I'm all right now and ready to party." She shook her shoulders as she moved across the room closer to him.

"I'm worried about you." He cast his gaze on her.

She was touched by the concern in his eyes.

"Before you woke up, you called for your mother," he told her, then tightened his lips. "I'm not sure why you called her Lillian."

Carly placed her hand on his cheek and caressed it. She looked into his eyes and held her breath. His revelation caught her by surprise.

"I wasn't calling for my mother." She turned away, faced the door, and dropped her hand to her side. "I was having a dream about our first baby. The one I lost when we were in college." She swallowed the lump in her throat. "I wasn't sure what her first name would be, but I knew her middle name would be Lillian, or Lilly, for short, after her grandmother and great-grandmother."

Mace turned her around to face him. "Why now?"

"I guess it's because of the incidents that could have hurt the child I'm carrying. First the incident outside the shop, then the nail gun disaster at the Renovate Charleston project." She looked down and encircled her belly with her hands. "Mothers are supposed to protect their children. I try not to think too much about it, but after last week, it has been unnerving."

"I understand, and I hope you understand my motivation." He focused his attention on her. "A father is supposed to protect his child too. The fact that someone would try to harm you, or any other woman, doesn't sit well with me. If I dwell on it too much, it flies all over me and I get angry."

"I hear you, but Mr. Chess Master, I've listened to your phone calls this past week and you're trying to move too many pieces on the board. You have your fraternity brother who owns a security business on surveillance tonight with his employees."

He ran his fingers through his hair. "They're also well-known members of the community. If I had too many of my security guys there, it would attract attention. This way, there's an increased likelihood that they'll blend in."

"Why do you think you need security if Simeon Clarke is one of the suspects? He was one of the first to decline the invitation."

"As I suspected he would." He lifted his chin so that she could straighten his tie. "I'm going to get more information from Nala, if I'm lucky, and her ex, Preston."

"Even though your brother thinks that you should leave the investigation to the authorities, you remain determined to pursue it. Is it your pride, a need to seek justice, or maybe vengeance?"

"I'm not going to lie." He bit his lower lip. "All of the above. Whoever was behind the attack sent me a message. I plan to respond. The attack on you and Yara got a lot of press coverage. There's no way I can let it go. I have someone at the police station, and they keep telling me that they don't have any clear leads." He made fists at his sides.

Their security system buzzed, alerting them that Ariel had been cleared to come up to their high-rise condo. She rang the doorbell. Mace walked across the floor to open the door.

"Hey, Ariel, come on in." He moved aside to allow her entrance to the front room.

"You look great." Carly came forward to hug Ariel.

She motioned for Ariel to twirl around so that they could admire her outfit. She was dressed in a purple satin dress that matched the purple mask finished with brocade material and feathers that covered her face.

"Love your dress." Ariel leaned back to take in a full view of Carly's outfit. "Where's your mask?"

Carly went to the table near the door and held up her mask of gold, purple, and touches of green made in a flare design that encircled her head like a crown. The mask covered her forehead and cheeks, giving her a look of allure and mystery.

"We can admire each other later." Mace grabbed his mask with its glossy embroidery in gold and purple, finished with warrior feathers and leather. "Make sure we stick to the plan. Carly, if she asks you about the terms of the settlement since she signed papers dropping her suit, string her along and tell her all you know is that it's still being worked out with the lawyers."

"Yes, sir." Carly saluted and laughed.

Ariel clicked her heels together and joined Carly laughing.

"Nala will probably drop her guard around you, Ariel. I was observing her with you at the renovation site. She wasn't as defensive as she is with—" The security system buzzed again, interrupting Mace's thoughts. He opened the door for Yara. "Hey, sis." He patted Yara on the shoulder. "Like I was saying, Nala is more defensive around Yara."

"Whoa." Yara held up her hands and looked at each of them as she came into the room dressed in a black tuxedo jacket atop slim, form-fitting matching pants. Her mask had a simple elegance. Made of black leather with intricate cutouts, the mask was inspired by the beauty of nature. Its leaf design framed her face. "What's with the consensus that I make her defensive? Wasn't that the same bitch who nailed you to the wall, Ariel?"

Carly and Ariel raised their eyebrows while Mace answered. "Let's be cool. You know your assignment, right, Yara?"

"Yeah, yeah." She sat on the couch. "Make nice with Preston, who has been so concerned about me, while you all work Nala. Oh, by the way, Mace, she doesn't care too much for you either. If you kept up with her social media posts, you would know that." She folded her arms across her chest.

"We'll leave in separate cars," he advised. "Carly and I will get to the ballroom at the convention center first. Ariel, you arrive next, and last…"

"But not least," Yara added, rising from her seat. "I come in and pimp Preston for information."

"Yeah, something like that." He rolled his eyes, then held out his hand for Carly. "Are you ready?"

"See you there." She looked over her shoulder and waved.

"Tata." Ariel smiled.

"Stay focused." Mace pointed at Yara.

"If I don't, you'll know it." She turned back her lapel, revealing the small microphone and its wires sewn into her jacket.

"Mace." Carly's jaw dropped.

"It will be all right." He ushered her out the door.

***

The masquerade ball was a dazzling spectacle of color and sound, a swirl of opulence filling the grand ballroom. Crystal chandeliers threw cascades of light over the guests, their reflections shimmering on the polished marble floor. Soft music floated through the air, a string quartet blending perfectly with the hum of voices and the clink of glasses. Mace and Carly stood in the reception line, greeting guests as they filtered into the event. Behind them, floor-to-ceiling drapes in deep burgundy and gold framed the entrance, setting the stage for an evening of intrigue.

"Thank you for inviting us," one guest after another expressed to Mace and Carly, each voice blending into the next.

"This is the social event of the season, 2.0. We really enjoyed your reception earlier this year," one of the guests remarked.

Carly smiled graciously, her eyes scanning the room as she leaned into Mace, whispering, "Leave it to Nala to be late so that she could make a grand entrance."

Just then, the crowd shifted its attention as singer Darren Rutland, a local celebrity, entered with his wife. Their arrival drew applause and cheers. The rich tones of his laughter melded with the music as he spoke with Mace and Carly.

"Are you planning on performing tonight?" Carly asked, her hands clasped in playful anticipation.

"How could I say no?" Darren chuckled. "Let me mingle a bit before you pull me onstage."

Mace signaled the waitstaff, and trays of champagne and gourmet hors d'oeuvres quickly glided through the room, ensuring every guest had a drink in hand. As the crowd's attention lingered on Darren, a few heads turned as Nala appeared at the entrance, unescorted and striking in her presence. The sleek silk gown clung to her like water, glinting under the chandeliers, her ornate Venetian mask drawing limited curious gazes.

Carly noticed the quick shift in energy. Despite her attempt at a grand entrance, the crowd paid little attention to Nala. "That was awkward," she mouthed to Mace.

Nala moved with slow, deliberate grace, her gown a deep emerald that shimmered with every step, feathers and crystals on her mask catching the light like jewels.

"She's trying to impress," Ariel murmured as she joined Carly in the line. "Good. She didn't plan to blend in."

Carly extended her hand to Nala. "Welcome."

"I wouldn't have missed this for the world," Nala replied, her eyes surveying the room as though calculating her next move. "Wow, this is quite the gathering of Charleston's finest."

"Yes," Carly responded, her smile measured. "Everyone involved in the Renovate Charleston project was invited."

"Of course," Nala said with a polite nod, her gaze wandering past Carly as if seeking a better target. She hadn't acknowledged Mace once.

Carly raised her hand, and in an instant, the waitstaff appeared with trays of champagne.

"Please, let Ronan get some shots of you," Carly suggested. "You raised the most funds for the project."

Nala's face lit up with a practiced smile. "Of course."

Mace watched as she was led away, a look of satisfaction creeping into his features. "Well played, Mrs. Moore."

"I told you she doesn't like you," Ariel quipped.

"And it looks like she's not too fond of you either, Attorney Dennison," Mace added with a smirk.

The tension between the various players at the ball was palpable, a web of glances and whispered words tightening by the minute. The room buzzed with conversation, laughter, and clinking glasses.

Carly, feeling the fatigue of the evening, leaned into Mace. "I could use a break."

"I've got you." Mace gently guided her toward a private room at the back of the venue, nodding to Ariel to keep an eye on things in their absence.

Once inside the hospitality room, Carly sank into a plush couch, elevating her feet and sipping from a cool glass of peppermint-infused water. She let out a sigh. "Refreshing."

Mace's focus, however, was elsewhere. Multiple monitors showed different angles of the ballroom. He fixated on a particular screen showing Yara dancing with Chance Baker, one of his executive team members.

Carly glanced at the screen. "Looks like the planning committee went all out. The ballroom is gorgeous."

"Yes," Mace replied absently, his eyes narrowing as he watched the screen. "But Chance isn't supposed to be that close to Yara. He's going to mess things up."

Carly raised a brow. "They make a cute couple."

Mace dismissed her comment with a wave. "This isn't about cute. He's crossing lines." His voice tensed as he watched Chance pull Yara close, whispering something in her ear. The hidden microphone picked up the murmur.

"What are you doing?" Chance's voice was a growl, low but audible. His lips brushed her ear.

"You've been acting like a caveman," Yara shot back, her voice icy as she tried to push away. "Let's not do this here."

"Let's do it now," Chance snapped, pulling her tighter. "You're practically naked under that jacket."

Yara's eyes flashed with anger. "I'm wearing a midriff top. Get over it."

Their exchange simmered, the air thick between them.

Carly glanced at Mace, who was already rising from his chair as he said, "I need to go out there."

"Wait." Carly pointed at the screen.

Preston had stepped in, smoothly offering Yara his hand. "Does the lady want to dance?"

"I'd love to," Yara replied, casting a dismissive look at Chance.

Mace sat back down with a grin. "Now it's about to get interesting."

Ariel entered the private room with a swift glance at her watch. "Are you two all right? People are starting to ask about y'all. Darren agreed to perform in about ten minutes." She sighed, shaking her head.

“The officers from the Renovate Charleston organization are helping me work the room. I told them Carly wasn’t feeling well.”

“We’re fine,” Carly replied, offering Ariel a tired smile. She patted the empty seat beside her, but Ariel remained standing, eyes sharp.

“Nala is working the room too,” Ariel added, lowering her voice. “She’s loving the attention. Where did you even find those men to dance with her? They look like they stepped out of a male model catalogue. I wouldn’t mind borrowing one of them.”

Carly’s lips twitched in amusement. “She’s definitely eating it up.”

Carly’s gaze returned to the screen where Nala waltzed gracefully, basking in the envious stares she was garnering. The sparkling chandeliers cast a golden glow, reflecting off her intricate mask and shimmering gown. She glided as though she owned the room.

“She’s leaving no crumbs.” Ariel snorted, crossing her arms, but her tone turned serious as she observed the fragile facade behind Nala’s smile. “I hope you know what you’re doing, Mace.”

Mace didn’t answer. His jaw tightened as he shifted focus, toggling to another camera view. The screen flittered, bringing into sharp focus Yara and Preston on the dance floor. Apprehension built as Mace turned up the volume, listening intently.

“Are you all right?” Preston’s voice was soft, filled with concern as his hand rested protectively on Yara’s lower back. The music swelled around them, a haunting melody weaving through the crowd. “It didn’t seem like you were enjoying yourself back there. Is he your boyfriend?”

Yara chuckled softly. “Boyfriend? What’s that?”

She leaned into him, resting her head on his chest, her eyes briefly meeting one of the hidden cameras before she turned away. Preston’s hand shifted, tightening slightly, pulling her closer. The ambient noise of laughter and clinking glasses faded into the background as they moved in sync with the music.

“That feels good,” she murmured, her voice barely audible as she melted into the warmth of his embrace.

From across the room, Nala’s narrowed gaze tracked their movements, her mask barely concealing the disdain in her eyes.

"She still loves you," Yara whispered. "Look at her."

Preston sighed deeply, his face clouding over. "She thinks she loves me. But I never loved her."

Yara glanced up at him, her expression unreadable. "I guessed as much."

Her fingers toyed with the lapel of his jacket, their movements slow, intimate. The pull between them was palpable, like a taut string ready to snap.

"She called me last night," Preston continued. "Drunk. Said her brother convinced her to drop the lawsuit, but she couldn't let it go. She admitted to attending Carly and Mace's reception, in disguise, after I called off our engagement. She thought Mace was trying to humiliate her."

"What?" Carly gasped from her seat, eyes wide.

Ariel's head snapped toward her, but Mace motioned for them both to stay quiet.

Preston's voice dropped, almost conspiratorial. "She believed Mace wanted to expose her, show the world that she'd been abandoned by yet another man. She cried the whole time on the phone. Her father was the only one who ever loved her, and since his death, she's been lost. I'm in naval intelligence, as you probably know. I told my superiors not to push for the marriage, but they didn't care. Maintaining my cover was all that mattered."

Yara's eyes blinked with sympathy, though she remained silent. Her gaze once again darted toward the hidden camera before she turned her face away, shielding her expression. Mace leaned forward, muscles taut, as he signaled in the band director's earpiece to stretch out the song.

"She said she could see the bond between Mace and his brother. It also surprised her how much Carly's brother appeared to adore her. When he walked her down the aisle, Nala realized for the first time that her own brother had never looked at her with the same affection. That broke something in her." Preston's voice cracked, his vulnerability stark in contrast to his usually polished exterior. "I've always known Nala was addicted to fame and fortune, but she's complicated. She's not evil."

"Complicated?" Yara's lips curled into a small smile. "Is that your nice way of saying spoiled brat?"

Preston chuckled, pulling her closer. "Maybe." His tone softened as he gazed down at her. "But enough about her. Let's talk about you. The tech wizard who hacked into my firewalls." His voice dropped to a near-whisper, a trace of admiration in his words. "I know it was you. I traced it back."

Yara raised an eyebrow, lowering her gaze. "I didn't mean to cause any harm."

"Why are you doing this?" he asked, eyes searching hers for answers.

Yara's voice trembled, her hands tightening around his. "I'd do anything for Carly, Mace, and Ariel. They're my family."

A glimmer of emotion passed across Preston's face. He gently cradled the back of her head, his fingers brushing against the microphone hidden in her jacket. "We should talk elsewhere. Too many eyes here. And ears." He glanced around, tugging lightly at her jacket's lapel, muting the microphone in the process.

Carly shot up from her seat, panic rising in her chest. "No, Yara!"

Ariel placed a calming hand on Carly's shoulder. "Stay calm. Mace has this under control," she murmured, but Mace's face darkened.

"This was not part of the plan," he muttered through gritted teeth, slamming his fist onto the table as they watched Yara and Preston leave the dance floor.

Suddenly, Carly's phone pinged. She read the message aloud:

Yara: *Don't blame Mace. This was my idea. I'll be all right.*

"She's in over her head." Ariel groaned, rubbing her forehead.

"Over her head again," Carly muttered, nodding in agreement. "Let's go."

Without hesitation, they gathered their things and headed back to the ballroom, anxiety thick in the air as they braced for whatever was to come next.

***

Mace, Carly, and Ariel sat at the head table, smiles in place, watching the awards presentation unfold. The president of the Renovate Charleston organization took the mic as emcee, and though the room buzzed with excitement, Mace's thoughts were miles away, stuck on Preston's cryptic words and Yara's decision to leave with Preston.

After intercepting Yara and Preston earlier on their way out, Mace had barely convinced them to stay. "Don't leave. We all need to speak," he'd said, his voice firm.

Yara had flashed a sly smile at Preston. "We're just stepping out to the hotel lobby," she'd murmured, as if testing how far Mace would push.

Returning to the moment, his eyes shifted back to Carly as she clapped politely while Nala approached the podium.

"Thank you to the Renovate Charleston organization and the Moore Investment Group for this honor," Nala said, her voice smooth but calculated. "It's been my pleasure to raise funds to improve communities here. Alongside the Moores, we've shown that when we collaborate, the sky's the limit."

Mace and Carly exchanged a glance. The words sounded right, but the subtext was glaring. Nala was up to something, her intentions far from pure. Carly's lips twitched as though she'd caught the silent message too. Mace's jaw clenched. Nala might have signed the legal papers ending the lawsuit, but it didn't mean she was finished playing games. His gut twisted. Trust was rule number one, and Nala didn't have his.

As Nala finished her speech and accepted the plaque, Mace felt a tap on his shoulder.

Chris Saunders, one of his top security officers, leaned in. "Yara needs to see you."

Mace's pulse quickened. "I have to take this," he said to Carly, raising his hand in a casual gesture.

She nodded, her smile supportive but tinged with concern.

Following Chris, Mace made his way down a long corridor, eyes locking on Chance up ahead, his arms flailing as he argued with Yara.

Mace slowed his pace, listening as Chance spat, "So, sugar daddies now?"

Yara crossed her arms, cool and unfazed. "Who I'm with is none of your business, Chance." Mace caught the storm in Yara's eyes as she added sharply, "Don't act all righteous with me. I know what you've been up to. Maybe your housekeeper needs to do a better job cleaning under the bed. I found panties that weren't mine."

Chance recoiled, his voice dropping to a bitter edge. "This isn't about me. It's about you with that older man."

Yara raised her hand, a slow deliberate movement, her expression daring him to challenge her further. As Chance opened his mouth to fire back, Mace stepped forward.

"Stand down, Chance." His voice cut through the friction like a blade. Chance turned to face him, but Mace's focus was solely on Yara. "You asked to speak to me?"

Chance shot a look of frustration at Mace before storming off, leaving them at the far end of the hall.

"Are you all right?" Mace asked, his tone softer now that they had some privacy.

Yara let out a breath, her defenses momentarily slipping. "Chance is… I don't know what his problem is. One minute, we're just friends, and the next, he's acting like I owe him something. It's exhausting."

Mace shook his head, a bitter laugh escaping his lips. "He's not good enough for you, Yara. You deserve better."

Yara's eyes narrowed, irritation flickering across her face. "I never thought…"

"He's great in business, but when it comes to loyalty, he's always out for himself. Trust me, if I had a blood sister, I'd keep her far away from him."

Yara blinked, taking in Mace's words. For a moment, the fierce mask she wore slipped. But she didn't dwell on Chance. Her voice dropped to a whisper. “Preston told me to ask you about the Sindell brothers—Paul, Grayson, and Jerrod.”

“Yeah, I know them.” Mace tilted his head. “Their father, Paul, Sr., came to my grandfather asking for a loan. He used their land as collateral but lost it when he couldn’t repay the loan. Years later, Paul, Jr. came into some money and tried to buy back the land, but my grandfather wouldn’t sell it. Why are you asking?”

“There’s a connection between the Sindells and Simeon Clarke. One or both are holding a grudge against you. It seems that Jerry Sindell was the one they identified as the guy who delivered the tainted lunch to Carly.”

“Jerry?” He frowned.

“Jerry is Jerrod’s son. Jerrod died from boozing it for many years.”

“Sorry to hear that. Jerrod was always the nicest one of the brothers. I used to spend time fishing with him when they came to visit my grandfather before things went sour between them.”

“Preston seems to think this is personal. More than just business,” Yara remarked.

Mace nodded, his jaw tightening. “I need to get to the bottom of this.”

Yara’s voice trembled, but her resolve remained. “Someone attacked me, Mace. They threw me to the ground like I was nothing. This isn’t just your fight. It’s mine too.”

Mace’s hands landed gently on her shoulders. “I’m sorry that happened to you. But, Yara, you need to be careful while I figure this out.”

She wiped away a stray tear, forcing a tight smile. “Thanks. I’ll catch up with Carly and Ariel later. I have to go.” She took a few steps toward the waiting area. “I promised Preston I would have a drink with him.”

As Yara walked away, Mace’s mind raced. He needed to return to Carly, but this web of grudges and betrayals was tightening. It was time to act, and fast, before the storm fully hit.

Chapter Thirteen

CARLY stepped out of her physician's office with Mace close behind. A stream of professional workers rushed by, their footsteps echoing off the sterile white walls. Pictures of newborns adorned the corridor, tiny faces wrapped in pink and blue blankets, some wearing soft beanies, others posing in outfits that made them look like storybook characters. The serene images seemed so distant from the storm building inside her.

"Wait, Carly," he called.

With her eyes glancing at the pictures of beautiful babies, she hurried ahead.

"I'm still mad, Mace," Carly said over her shoulder, her voice clipped, her lips pressing together into a thin line.

She turned abruptly into a small alcove, fists clenched at her sides. Mace followed, his chest tightening as he placed a hand gently on the small of her back. He stepped in front of her, blocking her exit.

"What did I do?" he asked, his voice low but edged with concern. His gaze wandered to a nearby photo of a baby dressed in an outfit resembling a lamb. "Isn't she cute?"

Carly's eyes darted to the photo, and despite herself, a small smile tugged at the corners of her mouth. "She's adorable," she murmured, instinctively placing a hand on her belly.

But the moment was fleeting, her frustration returning in an instant. She turned her gaze back to Mace, the fire in her eyes undeniable.

"You had to exaggerate, didn't you?" she hissed, stepping closer, her growing belly nearly brushing against his waist. "Telling my doctor I was more fatigued than I let on? That I was struggling with food, working too many hours, looking pale?"

"All true," he replied, wrapping his arms around her waist, pulling her just close enough to feel the warmth of his skin. "Did I make your blood work come back anemic? Did I raise your blood pressure? Or paint those dark circles under your eyes?" He pressed against her gently, voice barely above a whisper. "Can I help that I'm in love with you and our baby? Should I not be concerned?"

She leaned her head against his chest, her stiffness slowly melting under the weight of his words. "Women work and have babies every day, Mace," she said softly, though her voice cracked with the effort of holding back tears. "I was fine with a few weeks off, but then my doctor says, 'Let's prepare for three months of confinement and see how it goes?' Three months?"

Her voice broke as the tears fell. Mace, ever prepared, reached into his pocket and handed her a handkerchief.

"This isn't good for someone trying to secure tenure," she whispered, the weight of it all crashing down on her.

He tilted her chin up, forcing her to meet his eyes. "One step at a time, okay? We'll get through this together." He kissed her hand gently, his voice soothing but firm. "It's going to be all right, I promise."

They walked toward the front of the office, and Mace couldn't help but feel the stares, the silent judgment as they passed.

"I'm feeling a little out of place here," he muttered. "Didn't get the memo that my 'tribe' wasn't welcome." His eyes swept over the room, noting the absence of men amidst the sea of pregnant women.

Carly sighed, rubbing her tired eyes. "It's logistics. The office schedules women alone on certain days to fit more patients in. You insisted I be seen today, remember?"

He smirked, unable to resist. "Well, it was your tribe that got my tribe into this mess."

She rolled her eyes, but the corners of her lips twitched. "You're right, and you're welcome."

As they stepped outside, a young woman approached, waving with a broad smile. "Mr. Moore! Fancy seeing you here."

Mace squinted. "Emily Anne Bradley, right? Evan's client?"

She nodded enthusiastically. "That's right. I'm here for my five-month checkup." Her hand rested on her prominently swollen belly. "Nice to meet you," she added, turning to Carly with a warm smile.

Carly returned the smile, though her eyes revealed something unsaid. "Five months? Wow."

As Emily disappeared into the building, Mace glanced at Carly's noticeably smaller bump. "You're about as far along as her, aren't you?"

Carly bristled. "Babies grow at different rates. You can't compare."

Before she could step off the curb, Mace stopped her, his tone shifting to something more serious. "Stay put. Your confinement starts now."

He walked across the parking lot, the weight of his promise hanging in the air. The car's engine roared to life with a press of his key fob, the sound almost ominous in the quiet afternoon.

When they finally got home, Carly opened the door to find the condo spotless, too spotless. The air was unnervingly calm, the kind of calm that follows a storm, making her feel as if something unseen was brewing just beneath the surface.

"Marlena was here today?" Carly's voice wavered as she looked around the pristine space.

"She'll be coming regularly," Mace said, guiding her to the couch. His grip was firmer than usual, as if he were trying to anchor her to the present. "Doctor's orders. No heavy lifting."

"And if I forget the doctor's orders, will you report me for memory impairment?" she quipped, half-smiling, half-sighing.

Mace leaned back on the couch, propping his feet on the table as he gently swung Carly's legs across his lap. His hands moved instinctively to her belly, a gesture of reassurance and control. "Ariel and Sam knocked it out of the park with the Renovate Charleston project. I've made Ariel our liaison with them and the Moore Investment Group. They'll also take over the renovation of your parents' old home—under your direction, of course. I know how much that place means to you."

Carly's gaze darkened, a glimmer of suspicion crossing her face. "Yara called last night. Said she's tied up with an assignment for the next few months. Did you have anything to do with that?"

Mace's expression remained neutral, but there was a slight tension in the set of his jaw. "I don't know anything about Yara's project. Did she tell you what it is?"

"She was vague." Carly narrowed her eyes. "That's usually not a good sign with her. She said she'd keep in touch though."

Mace rubbed her belly again, a soothing motion. "You'll be plenty busy, growing our baby. Trust me, the time will fly by."

"Easy for you to say," Carly muttered, her voice tight. "Is there anything else you want to drop on me? Because I feel like the ground's shifting under me right now."

Mace hesitated, his eyes focused on a rolled-up white cylinder on the coffee table. "There's something I've been wanting to ask you for months. I'm not trying to start a fight, Carly, but we need to talk about your plans."

She crossed her arms, her lips pressed into a thin line. "I'm listening."

He unrolled the cylinder, revealing architectural plans. His movements were methodical, deliberate. "Before we get into these," he said, pointing at the plans, "I want to talk about your career. You've been chasing tenure for a long time. What does it really mean to you?"

Carly blinked, caught off guard. "What? You know that already. It means job security, financial stability, respect in my field."

He nodded slowly, his fingers tracing the edge of the plans as if grounding himself in the conversation. "I get that. But how much job security do you need? Enough to spend your life under constant pressure to publish, to worry about funding cuts? You've talked to me about your goals, your passion projects. What if there was another way?"

Her defenses went up instantly. "You can't buy tenure, Mace."

"I don't want to buy it," he replied, lifting her chin to meet his gaze. "But what if you didn't need it? What if you had the freedom to create your own think tank? To set your own agenda without answering to anyone? With the resources we have, you could hire your own staff and tackle the projects you care about without waiting for approval."

Carly's breath caught in her throat. "You've thought about this."

"Of course I have," he said, his voice steady, almost too calm. "I've talked to people—people who know how this world works. And they all said the same thing: tenure isn't what it used to be. The pressure, the lack of funding… it might not be worth it."

She rubbed the back of her neck, feeling the weight of his words sink in. "I don't know, Mace. This is… it's a lot to think about."

"You don't have to decide today," he said, sliding the plans closer. "But there's something else. My grandparents, Mason and Lucille Jefferson, left me a large piece of land on John's Island. I was thinking… with the baby coming, maybe it's time to build something for us. A home. An estate."

Carly's eyes widened in disbelief. "An estate? On John's Island? That's miles from downtown Charleston, away from Aunt Nora, my friends—everything I love about living here."

"It's not that far," Mace countered, his tone gentle but firm. "And it's not as rural as it used to be. We'd have more privacy and more space for our family."

"Mace, this is too much," she said, her voice trembling. "I can't handle all of this at once." She bit down on her fist, trying to steady herself.

Mace's phone buzzed, breaking the mounting strain. He glanced at it, his brow furrowing. "I don't expect you to make any decisions today." He stood and pressed a kiss to her forehead. "We're just talking. I need to take this call."

"Fine," Carly murmured, her eyes following him as he walked toward his home office. "I'll be here."

As he stepped out of the room, Carly felt the walls closing in. She heard Mace's low voice through the door, though the words were muffled. Her mind raced, replaying everything he'd said. Her career, their future, the estate—it was all spiraling too fast.

She'd seen the look on his face before he left the room. She had seen that frown many times. Something was up. Carly's mind swirled with unanswered questions. What was he really up to? And how much more was about to change?

***

Mace picked up his phone, activating FaceTime. "What do you have, Chris?"

"We're closing in on little Jerry. He fled to New York, and my informants are pretty sure that we've got him cornered. He and another man were the ones who roughed up Yara. We'll have him brought in for questioning. Do you still want to be present?"

Mace paced the room. "Carly was just told that she needed to go on medical leave. This isn't a great time to tell her I'm flying out on business."

"Let me know what you decide."

Another staff member came into the room with Chris, who was still on FaceTime. "We've located him, Mr. Saunders. We're going to the location now, and we'll transport him here at night through the service area."

"All right, I'll let you know." Mace ended the call and headed back to the front room.

Carly said, "I just got off the phone with Aunt Nora. She said she would love it if I could spend the night with her. We haven't had a girls' night to watch movies and talk in a while."

"Why are you planning a girls' night?" He cocked a brow.

"Because you've got to go out of town on business, and I'll be here since I can't travel. Am I wrong? I saw that look on your face."

He helped her get up. "No, you're not wrong." He pondered his options. "It should take less than two days."

"I was thinking that you would worry less about me if I was over at Aunt Nora's house."

"You're right." He smiled. "I'll be involved in intense negotiations, and I may have to shut my phone off for several hours. Are you okay with that?"

"I'll be okay. Starting now, I'll be a good girl and lie down while you pack."

He led her to their bedroom. "Did I tell you that you're a smart professor?"

"Not in the last hour. I have to go to the bathroom."

Mace waited until she had closed the door behind her. He took his phone out of his pocket to text Chris about his plans.

Get the jet ready. I'm taking the meeting with Jerry.

Chapter Fourteen

"I KNOW you've been waiting for news, but Jerry hasn't been as cooperative as we expected." Chris's voice echoed in the narrow, dimly lit corridor. The cold, concrete walls of the warehouse swallowed their footsteps. Every few paces, the low hum of fluorescent lights overhead flickered as though uncertain they wanted to stay on.

Mace remained silent, his jaw clenched. Jerry had slipped through their fingers for over a day, hiding until they'd finally cornered him in a grimy tenement on the outskirts of town. Now, Mace was about to get the answers he came for.

"Maybe you can make him talk." Chris halted at a rusted steel door and unlocked it.

Mace's black ball cap cast a shadow over his face, his eyes glinting in the half-light. He wore a fitted black shirt, black slacks, and designer sneakers—a sharp contrast to the grimy warehouse. He held up a hand when Chris offered gloves and a mask to hide his identity.

"I won't need them."

The door creaked open to reveal a stark room bathed in the harsh glare of a single spotlight. The rest of the space was swallowed by darkness. A table sat in the center, a metal jug of water gleaming under the light, and Jerry slouched in a chair, his wrists shackled. His eyes darted up as Mace entered, but when he tried to rise, one of Mace's men, built like a tank, forced him back into the chair.

“You can’t keep me here!” Jerry’s voice, high and desperate, cracked the silence, spittle flying as he struggled. His breath hitched, eyes wild as he scanned the room for an escape that wasn’t there.

Mace casually pulled a chair to the opposite side of the table, the scrape of metal legs on the concrete floor unnerving. He crossed his legs, settling in as though they were about to discuss a business deal.

“You’re right, Mr. Sindell.” Mace’s voice was calm, almost too calm. “This is America. The land of the free. But it’s also the land where you can’t attack women and walk away untouched.” He leaned back, the shadows swallowing his expression. “If you feel wronged though, I’m happy to call the authorities. They’re already interested in you. Fleeing South Carolina violated your parole, correct?”

Jerry froze, beads of sweat pooling on his forehead.

Mace pulled out his phone, deliberately slowly, and began dialing. “Nine… one…”

“Wait!” Jerry’s hand shot up, his knuckles white from gripping the edge of the table. Sweat glistened on his upper lip, and his breath came quicker. “What do you want?”

Mace didn’t flinch. “I want to know who ordered the attack.” His gaze drilled into Jerry, the temperature in the room seeming to drop a few degrees.

“I ain’t no snitch,” Jerry mumbled, attempting bravado as he wiped his brow with his sleeve. He leaned back, mirroring Mace’s posture, though his movements lacked confidence. The room seemed to tighten around him, each breath heavier than the last.

“Is that so?” Mace cracked his knuckles with a slow, deliberate pop. The sound echoed ominously. “What difference would it make if I tell everyone we got the information from you?” Mace leaned forward, his tone low and menacing. “We could start with how your uncle’s warehouses are used to move drugs from the Caribbean.”

Jerry’s body went rigid, fists clenching at his sides. Mace’s security detail shifted closer, their presence suffocating.

"I don't know nothing about that." Jerry's voice wavered as he stared at the looming men. "You might as well kill me. You know I'm dead if I talk."

"I'm not going to kill you, Jerry." Mace's voice dropped to a whisper, lethal and steady. "I just want to confirm what we already know. Was it your uncle Paul who set this up?" He slammed a fist on the table, the metal vibrating with a dull clang. The veins on Mace's neck bulged as he locked eyes with Jerry, his voice rising. "Or is family loyalty stopping you from admitting that he thinks you're worthless too?"

Jerry lurched to his feet, fury igniting in his eyes, but Mace's men held him in place.

"It was Leo." Jerry's voice cracked as he struggled, but Mace's men easily forced him back into his seat.

Mace smirked, inwardly pleased. He'd hit the right nerve.

"Who's Leo?" Mace pressed, but Jerry turned his face toward the ceiling, lips sealed.

Minutes crawled by in agonizing silence. The only sound was the steady drip of water somewhere in the darkness.

"If that's how you want to play it…" Mace's voice was slow, measured. "I'm not wearing a disguise for a reason. I want you to know exactly who I am." He stood, looming over Jerry. "Mason Moore. If anything happens to my family, to Carly, her friends, or anyone connected to them, you'll wish you were dead."

Jerry's eyes widened, panic flickering in his expression.

"And if you still don't want to talk…" Mace shrugged. "We'll just let the Feds take over. Or maybe we drop you back where we found you. I'm sure the people in that neighborhood would love to see your face again."

Jerry paled. "You can't do this! People will think I talked! I'll be dead!"

Mace ignored his plea and shifted his body away from Jerry, ready to leave. Pulling out his phone, he turned it on and immediately it buzzed with a message from Yara.

It's Carly. You need to come home. She fainted and was taken to the hospital. 911.

Mace's pulse spiked. He rose from his chair and turned toward the door with Chris on his heels. "Your choice, Jerry. It's all on you now."

As they stepped outside into the biting New York air, Chris turned to him. "What's going on?"

"Call Preston. Get Yara out of this mess." Mace's voice was clipped, eyes already scanning his phone for more messages. "From now on, deal with him directly."

Chris had to jog to keep up as Mace strode toward the waiting car, chest tightening with dread. Message after missed message lit up his screen.

"It's Carly," he muttered, panic creeping in. "Something's wrong."

Evan was also in New York on business. He abruptly rescheduled his meetings after Aunt Nora called to tell him that Carly had been taken to the hospital emergently and they couldn't find Mace. After Mace returned one of Evan's numerous calls, they arranged a rendezvous at the airport to return to Charleston.

Thump! The plane slammed into the runway, jarring Mace from his thoughts as it hit the ground with a hard, bone-rattling landing. The impact sent a shudder through the cabin, the sudden violence in stark contrast to the chaos brewing in Mace's chest. He clenched his fists, pulse racing, feeling every inch of the plane's grinding halt on the tarmac.

Evan, seated next to him, threw a glance his way. "I know you're anxious to get to Carly, but safety first, man. It won't help her if you don't make it because of a car accident." He unbuckled his seatbelt with a practiced calm, but there was a tremor in his voice, barely concealed under his usual cool demeanor.

Mace let out a slow breath, his head leaning back against the headrest. His insides churned with guilt and frustration. "I should never have left her." The words felt like gravel in his throat. "I knew something was wrong. She was pale, still sick. I ignored the signs."

"You couldn't have known," Evan said, trying to reassure him. "Carly's tough. She's made it through worse. Remember when Kate was pregnant? Morning sickness kicked her hard, but she fought through it. Carly will too."

Mace didn't respond, his mind racing to Carly, imagining her pale face, her frail body. How could he have left her? A gnawing sense of dread settled in his gut.

Suddenly, Andrew's voice cut through the cabin. "Boss, I've arranged for an escort to Henrietta Street. The security team's coordinating with local authorities."

Mace's jaw tightened. "Why Henrietta Street? She should be at the hospital."

"The hospital discharged her," Andrew explained. "Aunt Nora took her home. She's resting."

"Her home's not on Henrietta Street." Mace's voice lowered, eyes narrowing as he stared out the window at the gray clouds hanging ominously over the city.

***

Mace and Evan quickly left the private airstrip and climbed into their waiting vehicle, joined by an entourage of black SUVs surging through the city streets, lights flashing, horns blaring. The convoy cut a path through the traffic, racing toward the heart of Charleston. Mace sat in the back of the Escalade, his leg bouncing with impatience. Every second felt like an eternity.

"Mace, you need to approach this calmly," Evan said, loosening his tie. "There could be a reason why Carly's with Aunt Nora instead of home at the condo. You need to keep a level head." He placed a steadying hand on Mace's shoulder. "Are you hearing me?"

"I hear you." Mace's voice was tight, his focus trained on the blur of passing buildings. He tapped the back of the driver's seat. "Faster."

The driver caught his eyes in the rearview mirror, hesitating before Evan shook his head slightly. Mace swallowed his frustration, his mind drifting to the past—back to the first time he'd seen Carly.

He'd been in third grade, following her older brother, John, to check on her in the first-grade classroom. She had looked so small, sitting at her desk coloring. When she saw Mace, she smiled a radiant, innocent smile that stirred something deep within him even then. It wasn't love, not yet, but it was a desire to protect her, to keep that smile from ever fading.

Now that smile was a distant memory, replaced by the vision of her pale, sickly face. His heart hammered.

"We're here," Evan's voice cut through Mace's thoughts as the car pulled up to Aunt Nora's house on Henrietta Street.

Mace barely registered the blooming gardenias and neatly trimmed hedges as he threw open the door, rushing to the front steps. The air was thick with tension, each second dragging like an anchor around his neck. Aunt Nora opened the door, her face a mask of unreadable calm. She stood in the doorway like a sentinel, blocking his path.

"Aunt Nora," Mace forced himself to soften his tone. "I need to see Carly."

Her eyes lingered on him before she finally stepped aside. "She's resting."

Mace stepped inside, his heartbeat thudding in his ears. The smell of gardenias from the porch mingled with the scent of something cooking inside, but it didn't soothe him. His muscles were coiled tight, ready to spring.

"She just fell asleep," Aunt Nora said, wiping her hands on her apron. "You think it's wise to wake her?"

"I appreciate you taking care of her, but I need to take her home where she'll be more comfortable."

Aunt Nora's gaze hardened. "She's been worn down. I've seen her like this before."

"When?" Mace's voice sharpened.

"Ten years ago," Aunt Nora said, crossing her arms, her eyes gleaming with unspoken hurt. "When she lost you, and not long after, she lost her baby."

Mace recoiled as if he'd been struck, the words hitting him like a freight train. His throat tightened, the air suddenly too thick to breathe.

Aunt Nora's voice cracked. "I know that the baby she lost was your child."

Mace swallowed, his voice barely above a whisper. "I didn't know she was pregnant with our child when we were in college. She didn't tell me until last year, after we got back together."

"I don't blame you. She made us promise not to tell you," Aunt Nora said softly. "But understand, Mason, we had to pick up the pieces when she was too broken to move. She had to mourn you and the baby." Her voice faltered, tears threatening to spill.

Mace's chest ached with the weight of her words. "I wasn't there," he admitted, his voice low and filled with regret. "But I'm here now."

He stepped forward, opening his arms, silently pleading for forgiveness. She hesitated for a moment, then leaned into his embrace.

"Aunt Nora," he whispered. "I'm here to take her home."

Aunt Nora pulled back, studying his face for a long moment before nodding. "She's in the room down the hall. On the right."

Without another word, Mace strode down the hall, his heart pounding. Every step felt like a lifetime, each second stretching longer than the last.

"Please, God. Let her be okay."

He reached the door and hesitated. Then, from inside, he heard a soft voice—her voice.

"Mace? Is that you?"

Chapter Fifteen

CARLY sat up in bed, her head resting against the pillows, arms trembling as she propped herself on her elbows. Mace stood in the doorway, his chest tightening at the sight of her. She was five months pregnant, but her once-radiant glow had dulled and dark circles ringed her eyes. The fullness of her cheeks had disappeared.

It had only been two days since he last saw her, but the changes in her body, the weight loss, hit him all at once. She wore a T-shirt that seemed too large, the sheets pulled around her waist, her form much frailer since they'd returned from Barbados. His heart pounded in his chest.

"Carly." He moved swiftly to her side and sat on the edge of the bed. Her hand reached for his.

"I thought I heard your voice," she whispered, yawning. "I wasn't sure if I was dreaming."

"How are you feeling?" His voice cracked as he leaned forward, kissing her softly, his lips trembling against hers. "You scared me half to death." His eyes locked with hers, wide with fear. "They told me you fainted… found you in the car, unconscious."

She held him around the waist, her voice barely audible. "I didn't mean to scare you. I remember getting in the car to go to Aunt Nora's, then everything went black." Her fingers dug into his back, the feelings palpable between them. "I must've gotten dizzy."

"The baby?" His hand instinctively found her belly, his voice breaking with a mixture of hope and terror. "How's our baby?"

"The baby's fine," she assured him, placing her hands atop his, her lips trembling as she tried to smile. "They ran all the tests. Everything looks good."

He exhaled sharply, relief flooding through him. "Thank God." He gently swung her legs over the side of the bed, her feet dangling inches from the floor. "Let me help you get dressed."

"They tried calling you." She looked down, avoiding his gaze. "But your phone must've been off. I didn't want to worry you until we had answers. It took some time for the results to come back."

His jaw tightened. The thought of her suffering in silence made his blood boil, a mixture of guilt and anger swirling inside him. But before he could respond, a soft knock on the door pulled their attention.

"I'm in the kitchen if you need me," Aunt Nora said quietly, closing the door behind her.

"It's late," Carly whispered, her hand gently cupping his cheek. Her eyes, usually so bright and defiant, were now pleading. "I promised Aunt Nora I'd stay the night."

Mace pressed his forehead to hers, his breath hot against her skin. "I'm here now. Let me take you home. I can take care of you." He captured her hand, pressing it firmly to his chest, where his heart pounded relentlessly. "Am I wrong for wanting you home, safe with me?" His voice was low, edged with desperation. "For wanting to wake up next to you, knowing you're okay?"

Her hand trembled in his, eyes glossing over with unshed tears. "No, Mace. You're not wrong." She shook her head, her voice quivering. "But I'm so tired. I just want to rest for tonight."

His jaw clenched as he fought the rising tide of emotion. "If you're too tired to get dressed, I'll wrap you in this sheet and carry you out myself." His eyes bore into hers. "I'll call Marlena, and she can take care of everything around the house. I'll also call the school and have them cancel all your appointments. You'll have nothing to worry about. Just tell me what you need."

"I just need to be still," she whispered, pressing her head to his chest, her exhaustion weighing down every word.

He stood, unfastening his tie with a resigned sigh. "All right." His voice softened as he unbuttoned his shirt. "Then I'm staying."

"Mace—" She started to protest, but he shook his head, his decision made.

"No." He kicked off his shoes and climbed into the small bed beside her, the mattress creaking under the weight of both their bodies. "I'm not leaving you." The bed was too small for both of them, their limbs tangled awkwardly, but he didn't care. He pulled her close, wrapping her in his arms as if shielding her from the world. "I got you, Carly. I'll always have you."

She opened her mouth to object, but he silenced her with a kiss, slow and tender. His hand traced down her body, every touch a reminder of the bond they shared, the life growing inside her. He kissed her neck, his lips brushing against her pulse.

"You want me to go now?" His voice was a soft, teasing whisper.

She shivered, her breath catching. "No," she managed, her voice barely audible. "Stay."

His kisses deepened, moving slower, more deliberately. "I'll take care of you." His voice, low and husky, filled the dark room. "Lie still, let me take care of you."

The hours melted away in the warmth of his embrace, fear momentarily forgotten.

The next morning, sunlight spilled into the kitchen, casting a glow over the well-loved space as Aunt Nora stirred at the stove, her apron tied tightly around her waist.

"Good morning, Carly," she greeted her warmly without turning.

The smell of sizzling bacon filled the kitchen, thick with the warmth of Aunt Nora's touch. Mementos from past travels adorned the refrigerator, each souvenir like a bookmark in the novel of family history. But today, the comfort was thin, almost fragile, as if one wrong move could shatter it.

"Did you rest well? I can't remember the last time you slept in like this." She wiped her hands on her apron and turned to Carly with a knowing smile. "Mace still sleeping?"

Carly stretched, feeling the weight of a restless night pulling at her limbs. "Yeah, he's still out."

She offered Aunt Nora a soft smile before making her way to the fridge. The familiar coolness of the door handle grounded her for a moment. Dressed in one of Aunt Nora's oversized robes, she leaned in, searching for the pitcher of peppermint tea. Anything to keep the nausea at bay.

"That tea really worked wonders yesterday," Carly muttered, pouring herself a glass and closing the fridge, her eyes catching a crayon drawing of a house, a tree, and a rainbow arched into a heart. A child's scrawl beneath read: *To Grandma, from Nicole*. "How old is Nicole now?"

"She's six," Aunt Nora said, gesturing for Carly to sit at the large oak table that had always welcomed laughter and conversation. "I made a breakfast casserole just for you. Egg whites, peppers, and a few spices. Pregnant Woman's Delight, I call it." Aunt Nora winked, placing the plate in front of Carly. "I used to make this for your mama when she was carrying you. She had morning sickness for months too."

Carly forked a small bite and tasted the comforting blend of eggs and vegetables, closing her eyes as the flavor washed over her. "This is so good," she mumbled between bites, her mood lifting for the first time in days.

The sound of Aunt Nora pouring her a fresh glass of tea made the moment feel homey, safe, yet there was an underlying tension, an unspoken truth simmering beneath the pleasantries.

Aunt Nora took a seat beside her. "You're carrying a life now, Carly. It's not just you anymore." Her voice wavered ever so slightly, a hint of concern creeping in. "But I know you, child. You'll be a good mama." She gave Carly's hand a firm squeeze before pulling away, her face carefully neutral.

Carly felt the weight of Aunt Nora's words, the warmth of her hand still tingling against her skin. Her fingers drifted to her belly, but the motion wasn't the familiar, hopeful touch she had come to expect. It was laced with doubt. Fear. Her eyes glanced toward the door as Mace shuffled in, still wearing yesterday's clothes, his shirt untucked and rumpled. He stretched, yawning, but his eyes held the same fatigue she felt in her bones.

"Talking about me, I hope," Mace teased with a sleepy grin, trying to bring some lightness into the room as he slipped an arm around Carly's waist.

Her body stiffened for a second before she leaned into him. "Always," she murmured, but even her voice lacked its usual warmth. She knew something, not just *business,* had happened in New York. She just wasn't sure what had taken Mace's attention for hours.

Mace sensed the energy shift, pulling back slightly to look at her. "You okay?" His brow furrowed, his concern deepening as he watched her carefully.

Before Carly could respond, Aunt Nora placed a plate piled high with food in front of Mace. "Sit and eat. You need your strength too, you know." She offered a quick smile, but her eyes darted between them, picking up on the storm brewing beneath the surface.

The quiet clatter of forks and the steady hum of the kitchen could no longer mask the discord building between Carly and Mace. His eyes focused on her, searching for answers she wasn't ready to give. Carly avoided his gaze, choosing instead to stare at her plate, her thoughts a tangled mess of fear and frustration.

"I'm staying here," Mace said quietly but firmly, as if the decision had been made long before this conversation. "Wherever you are, I'm there."

Carly's hand tightened around her fork, the metal cool and rigid against her palm. She spoke softly, but there was an edge to her words. "I'm feeling better, Mace. I can go home, and you can go back to work. We can go back to our normal life—our bed, our routine."

Aunt Nora tried to change the mood by offering light-hearted comments about neighbors calling about the SUV caravan of Mace's employees blocking the street. But even her humor couldn't cut through the friction simmering beneath the surface.

Mace's jaw clenched. "This isn't just about normal life anymore. We have to think about your health and the baby, Carly."

The room seemed to close in, the air thick with the weight of decisions that would change everything. Carly's pulse quickened. The future she had imagined with Mace, the perfect balance between career and family, now seemed so fragile.

She rose from the table, needing space, needing air. "I know what's at stake, Mace, but I can't stay in this bubble forever. I need to work, even if I do it at home. I need to feel like me again."

Mace stood, his voice low but filled with urgency. "I understand, but our careers aren't as important to me now. What if something happens to you or the baby? I don't know if I could survive that."

Her heart pounded, the thud drowning out the distant sound of the kitchen clock ticking. Each second felt like a countdown to a decision she didn't know how to make. *Wasn't it him who was out of the loop for hours, taking care of business he chose not to share with me?*

The smell of bacon, once comforting, now clung to the air, heavy and stifling.

Carly's eyes filled with unshed tears, the room blurring around her. "I don't want to lose myself. I don't need you to say how devastating it would be to lose our child." *Not again.*

His hand reached for hers, but she pulled back, stepping away as the emotions churned between them like a rising storm. The threat of loss loomed large, not just of their child, but of everything she had worked for before they'd reconciled.

"I love you, Carly," Mace said, his voice thick with emotion. "But we need to be smart about this. I made a commitment to you, and for me, our family comes first."

She shook her head, the tears spilling over. *Was he asking her to choose between their family and her career?*

The vibe in the room shifted again as she looked at Mace. The turbulent look in his eyes was unsettling, betraying his attempt to remain calm.

"Let's keep it light," Aunt Nora said, trying to lower the temperature in the room.

"Things have happened in the past few weeks that have added to your stress. I know it's not just your job. I promise I'll do anything to keep you and the baby safe." Placing a hand in the arch of his back, Mace stretched out his sore muscles. "I'm going to finish this feast, then go home and change. Carly, if you feel more relaxed staying with Aunt Nora for now, I'll pick up some clothes and toiletries for both of us before I return." He resumed filling his mouth with food.

"That's not necessary." Carly tightened the tie around her waist to close her robe. "The bed here is too small for us and…"

"Babe, we've discussed this already," he said with a small frown. "I'm staying wherever you stay."

"That's the point." She placed her hands on the table. "I'm feeling better, and I need to go home to be with you, my husband, and sleep in my own bed."

Aunt Nora placed a mug filled with hot black coffee on the table in front of him.

He lifted the mug to sip his coffee and to hide his smile. "So, we'll be leaving soon?"

"You don't have to look so upset." Aunt Nora pursed her lips with sarcasm. "I don't need all this food to go to waste. I'll call in the guys in your entourage to eat while Carly gets her things."

"Give me a few minutes to get dressed and gather the few things I have here. We can talk more when we get home."

Carly looked at Mace, and before she turned to leave the room, he blew her a kiss and mouthed thank you.

Chapter Sixteen

THREE months later.

Mace sat back in his chair, the early morning sun casting a golden hue over the Cooper River. "Has it really been so bad, staying home with more time to call your own?" he asked, his gaze lingering on Carly as she chewed her toast.

Carly shielded her eyes from the sun with a hand. "No, it hasn't been as bad as I thought. I like starting the morning with you, watching the sunrise, welcoming the daybreak. You've always been an early riser." A smile tugged at her lips, warmth passing between them.

"I like getting a head start," he said before wiping his mouth with a napkin and placing it on the table. "Before the stock markets open, I get to see what's happening around the world." His voice was steady, but there was a hint of something more, something unresolved. "And today, since I'll be working from home, I think it's a good time to revisit something I brought up months ago."

Her brow furrowed, curiosity creeping into her expression. "What is it?"

He leaned forward, his hand reaching for hers, thumb tracing the delicate skin of her wrist. "First, have you thought about my proposal to start a think tank?"

"Mace..." she said, her lips parting, but he gently raised a hand, stopping her from answering.

"Let me finish," he said, his grip on her hand tightening. "I can't understand why you have trouble accepting money from me. I'm your husband. My money is your money, Carly."

Her gaze was brief and filled with hesitation. The tension between love and independence tugged at her heart. "It's not that I don't appreciate it, but what if we disagree on something? What if the think tank doesn't support the position your company wants me to take? What then?"

His lips pressed into a thin line as he considered her words. "I get it," he said, rubbing his chin thoughtfully. "But that won't be a problem. The money would be yours to use as you please. If that doesn't feel right, there's another option." His voice dropped, laden with vulnerability. "You could use the money my grandfather left for you."

Her breath caught in her throat. "What? Why would he leave me money? We weren't even together when he died."

Mace's eyes clouded, shadows of the past haunting his expression. "He left it in an irrevocable trust. I found out when I went through his papers. He contacted you back then, didn't he? To write to me?"

Carly's heart thudded, memories of that time flooding back like a dam breaking open. "I didn't write to you because I couldn't agree to what he wanted."

He searched her face, confusion mingling with hope. "What did he want?"

Her voice dropped to a whisper, a confession long buried. "He wanted me to tell you I'd moved on. That you should do the same."

He blinked, the air between them thickening with unresolved pressure. "Isn't that what happened?"

Carly's hand trembled as she reached out, fingers brushing his. "He wanted me to say I didn't love you anymore." She looked him in the eye, her voice raw and vulnerable. "I couldn't say it, Mace. I couldn't lie. I never stopped loving you."

Time seemed to freeze as her words sank in. Mace pushed his chair back and pulled her into his lap, wrapping his arms tightly around her, as if holding on would keep the world from breaking apart.

"I never stopped loving you either," he murmured before pressing his lips to hers.

Their kiss deepened, his breath mingling with hers, the taste of morning coffee lingering as he caressed her back, hands roaming her waist, and a fire ignited between them—one built on passion, loss, and the enduring love that refused to fade.

When he pulled back, breathless, he gazed at her with wonder. "How did I get so lucky, after all this time?"

Carly rested her head against his chest, feeling the steady beat of his heart beneath her ear. "It wasn't luck," she whispered, her hand drifting to her growing belly. "We were meant to be. Meant to be a family."

Mace's hand joined hers over the curve of her stomach, his eyes bright with emotion. "Speaking of our family," he said, his voice a little hoarse, "what do you think about building a home on the land my grandfather left me? On John's Island."

Carly's lips tightened, uncertainty clouding her face.

He brushed a curl from her cheek, his fingers lingering. "Come with me today, take a ride out there. It's been a while."

She glanced out the window, a small smile breaking through her doubt. "It is a pretty day. All right, deal."

***

They decided to drive Carly's Audi. Mace slid on his sunglasses as he took the wheel. Heading for John's Island, they drove along the scenic route, following Maybank Highway to Bohicket Road. His grandfather had once told him how the island had gotten its name from English settlers who arrived from Barbados, a story that always brought a smile to his face. As they cruised, Mace opened the sunroof, allowing the coastal breeze to fill the car and lifting Carly's spirits as they headed toward the laid-back island, known for its peaceful, down-home charm.

"This was a good idea," Carly said, placing her hand on his. "This area has always been so gorgeous and peaceful." She smiled, gazing at the oak trees lining both sides of the road. The massive branches draped in Spanish moss created a green canopy, filtering the sunlight in a soft, golden glow.

"The locals call this area the Alley of Oaks," Mace explained, his voice laced with nostalgia. "It's always reminded me of a natural cathedral built by time. There's something spiritual about it."

Carly nodded, turning to admire the lush greenery. "I can see why this place means so much to you," she said softly, squeezing his hand.

As they continued, they passed by quaint restaurants and hidden shops, Charleston's best-kept secrets tucked away in the heart of John's Island. After about thirty miles, Mace turned onto a winding driveway that led them between old graves and crumbling headstones. The sight caught Carly off guard.

"Where are we?" she asked, looking around at the weathered stone angels and carved headstones just beyond the wrought-iron gates.

Mace cut the engine and turned to her. "This land belonged to my grandparents, but no one from my family is buried here."

Carly's brow furrowed. "Wait, then whose graves are these?"

Mace got out of the car and quickly walked around to her side. As he opened the door and offered her a hand, she slid her feet into her shoes, taking his hand as she stepped onto the uneven ground.

"The Sindell family," he said. "My grandfather received the land as collateral from Paul Sindell the second who didn't repay a loan he received from my grandfather. His sons tried to buy it back, but the sale was never finalized before my grandfather passed. They were never able to reclaim it."

They walked slowly, Carly careful not to trip as Mace led her toward a well-maintained family plot, where the name "Sindell" was etched above a brick-masonry arch. Carly studied the headstones, her brow still creased with curiosity.

"So, the Sindells aren't your family, but you maintain their plot?" she asked.

Mace nodded, glancing at her as they reached the largest headstone, which bore the name Paul Sindell. "My grandfather respected Paul Sindell the first, even though the younger generations were… less reputable. Out of that respect, he made sure their family plot would always be taken care of."

Carly traced the cool granite of the headstone, her fingers brushing the engraved letters. The air around them was calm, punctuated only by the sound of birdsong and the breeze rustling through the moss hanging from the old oak trees. It was as though time had slowed in this place, leaving only nature and memory.

Carly placed a hand to her forehead to shield her eyes from the sunlight.

"I've seen all I need to see." Mace looked at Carly. "My grandparents' farm is less than a mile from here." He turned and led her back to the car.

"You have more surprises for me today?" She walked along the path beside him.

"Always, my love." He pulled her close and kissed her temple. "I hope you enjoy it." Mace smiled, his eyes full of love and excitement.

Back in the car, they drove through another gated entrance, where Carly's eyes widened. "This is the Jefferson family farm?" she asked, her gaze sweeping over the expansive property, dotted with construction trucks and shaded by a canopy of leafy trees. "It feels more like an estate."

Mace chuckled. "It started as a farm, but over the years, it became something much larger. My grandparents expanded it bit by bit. The land has always been the heart of my family."

They drove up a long, winding driveway toward a large house, fountains bubbling near the entrance and construction noises filling the air. Mace parked and turned to Carly.

"I'm having some renovations done," he said, getting out to help her. "I thought seeing it in person might give you a better feel than just looking at the blueprints."

She smiled at him as she stepped out of the car, her gratitude clear. "Thank you for always thinking of me. It's been tough these last few months, but you've made everything easier."

Mace's gaze softened, and he wrapped an arm around her waist, leading her toward a white-painted gazebo nearby. "This is our journey together, Carly. I'm just trying to make it as comfortable as possible for you."

They reached the gazebo, where a table was set with flowers, silverware, and a catered lunch. The ceiling fan whirred gently, stirring the warm afternoon air as they sat down. Mace unpacked a fresh salad for Carly, topped with grilled chicken, and an assortment of fruits and breads.

"You really do think of everything," Carly said, her hand resting on his. "I don't know what I'd do without you. With the pregnancy, I've had to slow down so much, and you've been so supportive." She paused, her eyes filled with emotion. "Thank you for making this time feel like a mini vacation."

Mace kissed her temple, his love for her evident in every touch. "I promised you we'd do this together. This is our journey, and I wouldn't have it any other way."

As they ate, the sounds of the fountains nearby mixed with the rustling of leaves in the breeze. Carly savored each bite of her meal, feeling a sense of peace that only Mace could bring.

"I've been thinking," she said between bites, "about starting that think tank we discussed. Some of the people interested are international, so I understand now why your late meetings are important even when they're inconvenient."

Mace's eyes lit up. "You're sure about this?"

"Absolutely," she said. "I can manage my appointments, and I want you to keep doing what you're passionate about. We're building a future together."

He smiled, reaching out to touch her belly. "We're in this together, no matter what," he spoke, his expression filled with conviction. "And I know that no matter how much things change, our love is constant."

Carly smiled with her whole face filled with gratitude. She followed his gaze to a smaller wooden house in the distance, surrounded by a garden of roses. "What's that?"

"That's the original family home," Mace said, standing and offering his hand. "Come on, let's take the golf cart and I'll show you. I think you'll love it."

***

Mace opened the heavy wooden door flanked by green topiary plants on the porch. The railings were adorned with flowerpots, and a bronze-encased light fixture with a soft gas flame gave off the unmistakable charm of old Charleston. As they stepped inside, Carly's eyes widened in delight. The home, while much smaller than the sprawling mansion that anchored the property, felt warm and welcoming. Every inch of it radiated peace. The white cotton curtains swayed gently with the breeze, adding to the serene atmosphere. The upholstery, a soothing blend of white and light blue, invited relaxation. Beyond the front room, she saw a cozy breakfast nook and a space perfect for a study. She wandered down the hallway, noting the four bedrooms tucked quietly in the rear.

"I absolutely *love* this," she said, slowly spinning in a circle to take in every detail.

Mace smiled, watching her soak in the surroundings. "Wait a minute."

He placed his hands on his hips, but before he could stop her, Carly was already exploring. She moved toward a curio in the corner, filled with old family photographs. One in particular caught her attention—a black-and-white image of an older couple sitting on a porch with a young boy between them, dark curls framing his face as they both kissed his cheeks.

"These are your grandparents, aren't they? And this adorable little boy… this has to be you!" she said, her voice full of affection as she smiled at him.

Mace gave her his signature shy grin. "Yes, that's me with my grandparents, right here on this very porch." He pointed toward the front of the home. He tucked his hands into his pockets, clearing his throat. "But there's something else I really want you to see." He gestured toward the dining area, where a set of blueprints lay spread out on the table. "I've been working on these plans for the big house, and I want your input. Take a look at how I'm redesigning the entrance. There's also plenty of space for a growing family."

He turned a few pages, revealing plans for the second floor as Carly leaned in closer.

"I think we'll be as happy here as my grandparents were," he said quietly, a mixture of hope and vulnerability in his voice as he watched her pore over the designs.

Carly took her time, studying the blueprints for their future home. One page after another, she absorbed the plans Mace had meticulously crafted.

"And look here." He pointed at a particular room. "There's a library, just for you. You can design it any way you like. I thought seeing the plans in person might be more exciting than just looking at blueprints."

Carly, her eyes still roaming the pages, paused. Her gaze shifted to the window, where a quiet courtyard beckoned. A large pecan tree stood majestically, shading the bricks.

"What's wrong?" Mace asked, noticing the moisture gathering in her eyes.

Carly placed a hand over her mouth. "That pecan tree reminds me so much of the one in my childhood home. My father made a swing for me, and I spent hours there as a girl. It was destroyed in a storm, but the memories… they're still so vivid."

Mace placed a comforting hand on her back. "I didn't know that."

She straightened her shoulders, wiping a tear from the corner of her eye. "I'm excited to see the main house. Let's go."

Together, they toured the large mansion under renovation, moving from room to room, with Mace showing her the extensive work being done while allowing time for her to rest. Afterwards, they returned to the gazebo, where a cooler filled with bottles of water and ice awaited them.

"I needed this," Carly said, sinking into a chair and taking a long drink of water.

Mace sat beside her, draining his own bottle before setting it down. "So, what do you think?"

Carly took her time, tapping the bottle in her hand as she considered her words. Finally, she turned toward him, her eyes fixed on his, wanting to convey her thoughts without hurting him. "Mace, you've thought of everything. This will be an incredible place to raise our family."

He looked away, bracing himself. "But…?"

She scooted closer, taking his hands. "You haven't told me much about your inheritance."

He quickly interjected, "*Our* inheritance."

"Yes, ours." Carly nodded. "I understand your grandparents chose you over their three daughters and your siblings to inherit this land. That couldn't have been easy for anyone."

Mace squeezed her hands. "If you're worried about legal issues or something happening to me, don't be. We've worked it all out as a family. The land will pass to you and our children. Years ago, I had the property appraised and gave my family their share of its monetary value. They appreciated the gesture, even though I wasn't obligated to do it."

"That's generous, Mace, but my concern isn't just legal. It's personal. I love Aunt Nora, and I like being close to her. She's getting older, and this place is a long drive for her."

Mace didn't miss a beat. "We can have a driver bring her out here anytime. I'll make sure it's not a problem for her."

Carly bit her lip, thinking. "I also know myself. I don't want to live in a mansion so big that we could all be under the same roof and still feel like we're living separate lives." She stood, her gaze drifting back to the smaller home they had visited earlier. "I think the reason your grandparents never tore down the original house is because it holds so many memories. I could feel the love in that place the moment I stepped inside."

She turned to face him, a new resolve in her eyes. "What if we use the larger house as a corporate retreat for your employees and as a place for big family gatherings? But for us, *our* family, I'd prefer us to use the smaller home for weekend getaways. I still love our home in the city."

Mace stared at her for a moment, then sighed and, with a soft smile, answered her. "I don't think I'll change your mind, will I?"

She shook her head, her expression tender but firm.

"Give me some time to wrap my head around it," he said, pulling her close. "I didn't expect this, but we'll work through it."

She placed a hand on his cheek, her love for him clear in her voice. "We will. Because we're family."

Chapter Seventeen

MACE settled into his office downtown, the low hum of city life filtering through the thick glass windows. Today was meant to be quiet, a day away from home to give Carly the space she needed for her work. She had made it clear that the executive meetings at their home had become too disruptive, and he'd agreed to move them downtown. As he adjusted his headset for a call, he had no idea his day was about to spiral into chaos.

"Yes, Chris," Mace greeted his head of security. "What's the update?"

Chris's voice was taut with urgency. "You got time? It's about Preston and..."

Mace straightened, his instincts flaring to attention. "If it's also about Jerry Jr., I'll make the time."

Chris exhaled sharply. "They've lost him. Jerry has dropped off the grid since his release. Preston wanted to know if we were involved."

Mace frowned, gripping the edge of his desk. "Why would we hide him from the Feds?"

"I think they're just covering their bases. But there's more. Preston's team has been looking into the Sindells and their recent activities. They've ordered an unusual volume of cleaning supplies—way more than what's needed for their contracts. They suspect it's being used in the manufacturing of drugs, and the shipments are coming through the ports in Charleston and Savannah."

Mace's pulse quickened, the knot in his stomach tightening. "Go on."

Chris continued, "And Simeon… he's bought more property next to the Sindells' warehouse. There's been a spike in shipments of porcelain, glass, pottery, but it all seems suspicious."

Mace's jaw clenched. "I don't care about Simeon's business. My focus is on keeping Carly safe."

Chris paused. "Preston understands, but he wanted you to know about a call he got from Nala. It's… unsettling."

Mace rubbed his temple, a deep weariness settling in. "Spare me the drama, Chris. Make it quick."

"Nala's unraveling. She called Preston, drunk and emotional. She's mad at him because he's refusing to pay more bills from their doomed wedding. During the call, she rambled about how close you and Evan are and even mentioned John, Carly's brother. She used the word *adore* to describe how attentive he was to Carly. She admitted she went to your reception out of jealousy and afterward had a blowout with her brother, Simeon. Shit hit the fan when she told him that he was never the brother she needed. Preston said Simeon responded in anger, saying something, according to Nala, about growing up and being teased with the name 'Simba' because of her. He didn't like it, and it messed with his head."

"Damn." Mace shook his head, half-amused, half-exasperated. "What does Preston want me to do with that?"

"Just something to file away," Chris replied. "One more thing. We're spread thin and Yara gave our guys the slip. We still have eyes on Carly and your New York apartment, but—"

Mace's phone buzzed again. "Chris, I need to take this. It's Carly." Switching over, he forced a calm into his voice. "Hey, babe."

"Hey, love," Carly replied, her voice light, but Mace's guard shot up instantly. "I'm heading out to run a few errands and meeting a friend at Folly Beach. Before you say anything, I don't need your security tailing me today."

Mace's heart stuttered. "What do you mean by no security?"

"I'm fine, Mace. It's been quiet since the attack. You know that."

He leaned forward, his tone hardening. "Carly, you carry my heart and our child. Do you understand that? I don't want to take any chances."

She softened, her voice wavering. "You're so sweet. I'll be careful, I promise. But I need some normalcy today. I'll be back before you get home. Love you. Bye." She ended the call.

Mace's hand tightened around his phone. A heavy unease settled in his gut. His phone buzzed again, snapping him out of his thoughts.

"Andrew, I said hold my calls!" he barked.

Andrew's voice cracked through the speaker. "Boss, it's your brother. He says it's urgent."

Mace sucked in a breath and switched lines. "Evan, what now?"

"I'm on my way to your office. Preston just reached out. He wants us to meet Paul Sindell immediately. Says it's critical."

Mace frowned, tension crawling up his spine. "Why should we care about a meeting with the Sindells right now?"

"Because Preston believes they're about to break a major case, and Paul might have intel on what happened to Yara, Carly, and the student who died after leaving her office. He's agreed to meet under our terms, but we need to go now."

Mace swore under his breath, rising from his chair. "Fine. I'll alert Chris to contact Preston."

Chris's Escalade pulled up in front of Mace's downtown office, the sleek black vehicle gleaming ominously in the sunlight. Mace wasted no time climbing into the backseat. His eyes darted to the rearview mirror, where Chris gave him a sharp nod.

"We're following Preston's team to an undisclosed location," Chris said. "They've disabled our GPS, and we'll be off grid until further notice. No phones, no weapons for you or Evan while in the meeting."

Mace's stomach twisted. "And Carly?"

"Preston initially had men shadowing her without her knowing. He had to reassign them, since they hadn't seen any suspicious behavior or threats to Carly since the attack."

Mace's gut still churned, the bad feeling tightening like a vise. "She's at Folly Beach with no protection."

Mace's mind raced. He sent a quick text to Carly, his fingers trembling slightly.

Doing ok?

Her response came quickly: *Doing fine.*

Evan arrived and got in the car. Mace updated him with the information they had, including his concerns that Carly was no longer under loose surveillance by the Feds even though they believed that her suspicions about activity at Clarke's Imports Store were valid.

Evan patted Mace's shoulder. "We'll get out of this meeting fast, then you can get back to her."

As they drove, the city's bustle faded into the distance. The dirt road they turned on was rough, the SUV rattling as it hit deep potholes.

Finally, they arrived at a heavily guarded gate, armed men watching their every move. The air felt thick, oppressive, as they were waved through and directed to park in front of a squat, stone building with narrow, slit-like windows.

Mace stepped out of the car, his muscles tense and coiled. "Let's get this over with," he muttered, his voice tight with foreboding. The weight of the situation pressed down on him as he walked toward the building, each step pulling him deeper into uncertainty.

Chapter Eighteen

CARLY tapped the steering wheel lightly, her fingers keeping time with the rhythm of Jill Scott's sultry voice as it flowed through the car's Bluetooth. The sun glinted off the hood of her car as she cruised down Folly Road, its golden light bouncing off the trees that lined the way. The gentle breeze through the open sunroof tousled her hair, and she leaned back with a contented sigh, her sunglasses shielding her from the bright summer day.

She glanced down at her belly, secured safely beneath the seatbelt, and smiled. "Your daddy worries too much about us," she murmured, rubbing her hand over the curve.

The day was as perfect as it could be—warm, breezy, and full of possibility. As she crossed the bridge toward Folly Island, the sparkling water below caught her eye, creating a momentary flash of dazzling light.

"Life is golden," she hummed along with the radio, her voice slipping into her own made-up lyrics.

The serene atmosphere wrapped around her as she pulled into the parking lot of the BLU restaurant. Carly found a spot easily, which seemed like yet another sign of how perfect the day was. She locked the car and strolled inside, the cool air from the hotel lobby washing over her like a welcome respite from the heat outside.

But something shifted. A sliver of unease crept up her spine when the hostess greeted her.

"Are you waiting for someone before I seat you? Is your friend parking?" the woman asked Carly with a polite smile.

"Yes, I'm meeting someone for lunch." She frowned slightly, glancing over her shoulder. No Samara. "She's running late."

Carly tried to push aside the strange feeling. She opted to wait at the bar, knowing her friend would arrive soon. But as she settled into her seat, Carly caught a glimpse of someone moving in her peripheral vision. Nala. Her heart sank.

Not today.

Carly shielded her face with the menu, hoping to avoid Nala's inevitable drama. The bartender arrived with her frozen drink, but the icy concoction did little to cool the tension that was brewing.

"Carly!" Nala's voice pierced the air, drawing the attention of several patrons. She rushed over, her energy invasive. "I was just thinking about you. We need to discuss the photoshoot for the baby."

A sickening knot twisted in Carly's stomach. She turned to face her, eyes narrowing. "What are you talking about?"

Nala leaned in, her perfume overpowering. "Your husband agreed that my company gets exclusive pictures. It was part of the settlement."

Carly's blood ran cold. There was no way Mace would have agreed to that. She stirred her drink absentmindedly, trying to keep calm. "I don't know what you're talking about. Mace wouldn't—"

"Call him," Nala snapped, her voice rising.

Heads turned once more, the bartender and the manager both glancing over with concern. The manager came forward.

Carly's pulse quickened. She stood, gripping her glass. "No need to call him," she quickly responded.

The manager, sensing the tension, escorted her away from Nala.

"Thank you, I'll wait at a table." Carly looked over her shoulder as Nala stormed out, her heels clicking angrily against the floor.

Once seated, Carly exhaled slowly, trying to shake off the encounter. She checked her phone, the latest message from Samara flashing on the screen: *Sorry. In a fender bender. Won't make it today.*

Her heart sank. The nervous energy coiled tighter in her chest. Just as she began to type a response, two women approached her, holding books. They introduced themselves—Cassidy and Kayla, history buffs, fans of her work. But something about the interaction felt… off. Cassidy hovered too close, Kayla too eager. Carly forced a smile as she signed their books, but the unsettled feeling grew, like a storm gathering on the horizon.

Finally, they left, and Carly found herself alone again. She pushed away her half-eaten appetizer and decided to head to the Moore family beach house on Second Street. The thought of the quiet, serene space brought her a sense of calm. Mace didn't know she'd be there, and she liked the idea of surprising him later. With Samara's help, she was remodeling the home.

But as she stepped outside, a sudden wave of dizziness hit her. She paused, gripping the doorframe, steadying herself as the world spun slightly. The fresh air helped, but only a little. Something wasn't right. Pushing the thought aside, she climbed into her car and drove to the beach house.

The house stood quiet, nestled against the backdrop of the Atlantic Ocean, its soft blues and yellows inviting her in. Carly wandered through the rooms, snapping pictures for Samara. But when she glanced out the window, she saw a familiar figure walking down the driveway.

It was Kayla. The woman from the restaurant.

A cold shiver ran down Carly's spine. What was she doing here?

Kayla waved casually, her dog trotting beside her on a leash. "Carly, I didn't know you'd be here. Small world, huh?"

Carly blinked, her vision blurring again as her head swam. She leaned against the doorway, feeling her knees weaken. Panic surged in her chest. "Kayla…" Her voice was shaky. "Something's wrong."

Without warning, her vision darkened, and her body swayed. Kayla was suddenly at her side, her arm wrapped around Carly's waist.

"Let me help you," Kayla said, her voice too calm, too composed.

Carly's hand fumbled for her phone, handing it to Kayla.

"Call my husband," Carly whispered, her voice barely audible as her world teetered on the edge of consciousness.

Kayla took the phone, but Carly couldn't shake the creeping feeling of danger closing in.

Chapter Nineteen

THE vibe in the room was suffocating as Mace followed Chris and Perry, also on his security detail, into the cramped space where Preston and several agents waited. A wall of screens covered with live feeds of the property's perimeter cast an eerie glow over the sparsely furnished room. Mace's eyes swept over the scene, a narrow interrogation room visible on one monitor, a metal table and chairs the only furniture inside. The heavy air felt oppressive, thick with the weight of secrets about to be unearthed.

Chris and Perry's jackets opened to reveal their holstered weapons, a silent reminder of the potential danger. Mace and Evan stood still as agents patted them down, the cold efficiency of the search intensifying the sense that they were stepping into something far more dangerous than they realized. As their phones were taken away, Mace's pulse quickened.

Preston's voice was calm but firm as he approached. "Thanks for agreeing to this. Chris, you and your team can stay here while we talk to Paul and his lawyer. We've moved them into the interrogation room." His casual wave toward the nearby rooms did nothing to ease the knot forming in Mace's gut. "We're on the brink of something big. Paul's the closest anyone's come to turning on Leo, and he wouldn't speak without you and Evan here."

Mace frowned, pacing in short, tight steps. "I still don't understand what any of this has to do with me. I've never met Leo. Don't even know him."

Preston's response was cut short as the door of the interrogation room swung open. Paul Sindell sat there, his face pale and drawn, dark circles shadowing his eyes. He looked like a man on the edge, his nervous energy palpable in the small room.

Mace dropped into the chair across from Paul, his long legs crossing with deliberate calm. "Let's get this over with," he said, his voice low, devoid of any patience for pleasantries.

Mace's eyes locked onto Paul's, and for a moment, the only sound in the room was the steady ticking of a clock on the wall, counting down the seconds to whatever revelation awaited them.

Paul leaned into his lawyer, whispering something before the man pulled out a briefcase and spread papers across the table. "My client has an offer."

"Let's hear the information first," Preston said, his tone sharp. "It better lead to something actionable."

Paul's voice wavered as he spoke, his eyes darting nervously between Mace and the agents in the room. "I've got a recording," he muttered, his hands shaking as his lawyer handed over a flash drive. "From my nephew, Jerry. It proves Leo ordered poison to be placed in Carly Moore's food. The same poison that killed that student."

The blood drained from Mace's face as his heart pounded violently. The room seemed to close in around him, the walls too tight, the air too thin. Sweat beaded on his forehead, but he forced himself to stay composed, his voice steady.

"I want a copy of that recording," he demanded, his gaze switching to Preston before settling back on Paul. "Now tell me what you want."

Paul's hand trembled as he waved aside his lawyer. "This is personal," he rasped, leaning forward as if confessing a sin. "Your family and mine… we used to be neighbors. Good friends." His voice broke, thick with emotion. "My father lost our land to your grandfather after falling on hard times. He thought he'd get it back, but… he didn't. That land, it's everything to me. My ancestors are buried there—my mother. I need it back."

Mace's eyes narrowed, unmoved by the emotion in Paul's voice. The room felt colder, the silence after Paul's words chilling. He didn't flinch, didn't blink. His voice was ice. "Why now?"

Paul swallowed hard, his nervous energy returning as he shifted uncomfortably in his chair. "I tried earlier, but you ignored my calls. Then Leo… Leo changed everything." Paul loosened the collar of his shirt, beads of sweat now visible on his brow. "He's not who you think he is. Leo—his real name is Simeon Clarke." Paul turned toward Preston and his laugh rang out, bitter and hollow as if taunting Preston. "The same man you almost had as a brother-in-law. Imagine that. Your *almost* brother-in law is the drug kingpin you all have been looking for and you didn't see it. He was operating under your nose and calling you all fools at the same time."

One of Preston's men attempted to physically charge into Paul.

"Hey, hey." Preston stepped forward to restrain the man. He looked at Paul. "We'll see who has the last laugh. You'd better be prepared to surrender him to us or to spend a lot of time in prison. Your warehouses have been raided. We found some *things* before you were able to hide them."

Mace sat back with a slight smile. *Things are about to get very interesting.*

"Like I said, you'd better be prepared to deliver him to us," Preston repeated, his voice sharp with warning. "Or you're the one who's going to rot in prison."

Paul glanced nervously at the agents before turning back to Mace. "Leo is furious. He hates that Carly's research into the Charleston and Barbados cultural connection is shining a light where he wants darkness. She's a threat to his operation. He's not going to stop until she, and you, are out of the way."

Mace fought the rising tide of panic, forcing his mind to stay sharp. Carly was in more danger than he had ever imagined. His heart raced as fear gripped him, but outwardly, he remained still, calculating. He couldn't afford to panic. Not yet.

"He's coming for you, Mace," Paul whispered, his voice trembling. "Listen, I need to use the bathroom before I talk."

Chapter Twenty

CARLY woke slowly on a couch, her head swimming in confusion as she blinked at the unfamiliar surroundings. The room around her, though decorated in soft blues and creams with nautical decor, did nothing to calm the sudden surge of panic bubbling inside her. Her pulse quickened. *Where am I?* She pressed a hand to the side of her head, trying to focus her thoughts. The last thing she remembered was being at the beach house, then everything went black.

Her eyes scanned the room, and as her vision cleared, she saw Kayla standing nearby. The sight of her brought no comfort. In fact, Carly's stomach churned with unease.

"Kayla?" Carly's voice was shaky, low. "What happened to me?"

"You got dizzy," Kayla said, moving swiftly to Carly's side. "I brought you inside. This is my home."

Carly placed a protective hand over her belly, dread rising in her chest. Something felt off—way off. Her bag was beside her, and she reached for it, fingers fumbling inside as she searched frantically. "Where's my phone? Did I give it to you?"

"No, you didn't." Kayla's eyes darted away, avoiding Carly's.

Outside, the last orange rays of the setting sun slanted through the window, casting long shadows that seemed to creep ominously toward Carly.

A lump formed in Carly's throat. "Kayla, can you call my husband? My car keys are missing too." She glanced at the darkening sky, her anxiety spiking. "I must've been out for a while. It's getting late… he's going to be worried about me." She struggled to sit up, her heart pounding harder as her instincts screamed at her *something is 'very wrong.*

Kayla's previously helpful demeanor was gone, replaced by a cold distance. The warmth that Carly had briefly felt evaporated, and an oppressive silence fell between them.

Carly's breath hitched. Her eyes darted around the room again, searching for an escape route, but her body betrayed her as a wave of nausea rolled through her stomach. Panic clawed at her chest. *This isn't right. I need to get out of here.*

She leaned back, dizziness making the room tilt. "I'm not feeling well," she whispered. Her skin felt clammy, cold, yet her heart was racing.

Kayla looked at the door, a sudden tautness in her posture. Carly's eyes followed, and her stomach dropped as the doorknob turned slowly.

"What took you so long?" Kayla's voice, tight and accusatory, cut through the silence.

Nala entered the room with a casual stroll, her disheveled appearance and the faint smell of alcohol wafting from her making Carly's dread deepen. Nala slouched into a chair near the door, her eyes red and glassy, her movements erratic.

"Did you place the car in the rear of the property?" Kayla snapped, clearly irritated.

"Yeah, yeah." Nala waved her off dismissively and let out a yawn.

Carly's heart pounded louder in her ears. *Nala's here too?* She tried to piece together the situation, but her thoughts were muddled. A creeping fear settled in as she realized she wasn't just in a strange place—she was in danger.

Carly swallowed hard, her mind racing. *I have to stay calm. Think, Carly, think.* She shifted slightly on the couch, hoping neither woman noticed her subtle movement as she scanned the room for an escape.

"Why the hell did Cassidy think to involve you in this? You're useless," Kayla sneered at Nala. "I knew this would be a disaster."

Nala scoffed, her glassy eyes narrowing. "You're not exactly holding it together yourself." She pointed toward Carly. "She's the one who screwed everything up. If it weren't for her, we wouldn't be in this mess."

Carly's pulse spiked. The conversation felt as if it was spiraling, taking a dark turn she hadn't anticipated. Her breath quickened as the air around her grew thick with tension. Her nausea returned in sharp waves. *God, what have I gotten myself into?*

Kayla's voice dropped to a dangerous whisper. "I told you not to eat those brownies," she hissed at Nala. "Those were custom-ordered for me and Cassidy, not you. The treats were highly caffeinated, and marijuana infused, just the way we like them." Nala had joined the two women at a bakery not too far from the restaurant after her encounter with Carly. "You're really a light weight."

Kayla turned away just as Nala rose from her chair, shrieking at the top of her lungs. She pushed Kayla to the floor, who landed on her outstretched hands.

"You smell like you were drinking." Kayla huffed. "You're clearly every bit the screwup that your brother says you are. It's hard to believe you and Leo are related."

Carly continued looking around the room, hoping their conflict would allow her to escape. There was a hallway to the right and another room to the left. Her breath quickened as she continued to struggle with nausea.

"You all talk about Leo"—Nala made fists at her sides—"like he's some prophet, the wisest man on the planet. The truth is my brother, Simeon, is a thug and a bully. I called him after our meeting at the restaurant." She pointed toward Carly. "You were right. He lied to me. Mason didn't agree to let me have an exclusive for pictures of the baby."

Carly remained still. Nala hadn't asked a question, and she wasn't offering answers to someone drunk and high on whatever she had consumed. Nala needed to get something off her chest.

"Was it my fault that my parents named me Nala and him Simeon?" She moved to the side of the chair. "Was it my fault that the other kids started calling us Simba and Nala, like in *The Lion King*?" She threw her head back with sinister laughter. "He hated it. Years later, one of his friends—I think it was Paul Sindell—who said since he was a lion, he would call him Leo. Paul was one of the cool guys in school."

Nala shrugged, still dazed, and Carly's unease morphed into pure terror. She wasn't dealing with rational people. Nala was on edge—drunk, high, or both—and Kayla wasn't far from losing control herself.

Carly shrank back against the cushions as Nala's voice rose in a manic pitch. "You think you're so smart, don't you?" Nala's face twisted into something dark and unstable. "I just wanted what's mine!" She pointed wildly in Carly's direction. "Mason promised me!"

Carly's blood turned to ice. *Mason never promised her anything. She's delusional.* Fear gripped her, and she instinctively wrapped her arms around her belly. "Please, Nala," she tried to reason with her, voice trembling, "I didn't mean to upset you, I just..."

Nala wasn't listening. Her voice grew louder, more unhinged, until she pulled a gun from her waistband. The small black weapon wobbled in her hand as she cried and waved it between Carly and Kayla. "This is messed up. Carly, I never meant to hurt you. I thought we could be friends. How could you embarrass me in the restaurant like you did?"

Though overwrought with emotions, Carly decided to speak and offer a distraction. "I didn't mean to embarrass you." She held one hand in front of her and the other on her belly. "I'm sorry if I did. Please understand that as a mother, it's my responsibility to protect my child. I wasn't born into a life of fame and fortune. My child's privacy is important to me. You... you, of all people, understand how mean kids can be... right?"

"Yeah." Nala lowered her head in a moment of quiet reflection.

"My baby is innocent, Nala. Please let me go. I'm not feeling well." She pressed her hand against her stomach. "I need medical attention. Whatever you gave me could hurt my child."

"I didn't give you anything," she snarled and grabbed the top of a chair for support.

"Stay focused, Nala," Kayla said. "Remember, your brother loves you. He's paving the way for your success. It's necessary to get Carly out of the way. You've seen how Mason looks at you. He wants you, and he'll need you to help raise this child. You know that's what you want. He's a rich man. He can give you whatever your heart desires. Simeon is going to help you get that."

"Stay down!" Nala screamed at Kayla, who had slowly started to rise from the floor.

Kayla dropped back down, hands raised in submission, while Carly's heart threatened to burst from her chest.

Time seemed to slow as Carly stared at the trembling gun in Nala's hand, her body frozen with fear. The bile in her throat rose, and she dry heaved, her body shaking with terror.

"Please, Nala… I don't want to die," Carly whispered, her voice barely audible. Her hand tightened over her belly. *I have to protect my baby. Her thoughts raced.*

The sound of footsteps behind her made Carly's breath catch. Cassidy appeared, her own gun drawn, moving with lethal precision.

Pow!

A gunshot echoed like thunder in the confined room, and everything went still.

Chapter Twenty-One

"TELL me why Leo wants to hurt my wife?" Mace fought the rising tide of panic, forcing his mind to stay sharp.

Paul took a long, shaky breath, clutching the bottle of water as if it might slip through his fingers. The small interrogation room felt even more stifling now, tension thick in the air, pressing down on everyone. Preston, no longer pacing, was seated at the table, his eyes sharp and locked on Paul. Every word hanging in the air carried weight.

"To answer your question, Mace..." Paul deliberately took a sip of water.

The slight tremble of Paul's hand didn't go unnoticed by Mace, who sat motionless but alert. His entire body hummed with unease, but he refused to show it. Not here, not now.

"Leo wanted you out of Charleston, where he controls the narrative. After your wedding reception, the local press, paparazzi... they brought way too much heat. This town hasn't seen that kind of attention in years. And Leo, well, he thrives in the shadows. Your presence lit up everything he wanted to keep hidden. And that pesky wife of yours..." Paul's voice trailed off for a moment.

Mace's eyes narrowed, his jaw clenched. "Careful how you talk about my wife."

Paul's eyes blinked with uncertainty, but he pressed on. "He didn't like her poking around in Barbados, digging into the projects she's been involved in. Carly's too smart for her own good and Leo saw that. She was getting too close to uncovering the truth about his operation. He's been passing off imports from China as authentic Barbadian goods, marking them up, making a fortune. But she saw the patterns, started asking questions." Paul shifted in his chair, the pressure of the room clearly weighing on him now. "Her Renovate Charleston project has been driving up property values, messing with his bottom line. He couldn't buy up property for dirt cheap anymore. He needed things to go back to normal."

Preston leaned forward, his gaze piercing. "What business exactly are we talking about? Remember, everything you say is being recorded."

Paul's eyes darted to the microphone, then back to Mace. He wiped the sweat gathering at his temple with a shaky hand. "Drugs. Big business. Coming in from the Caribbean through the Charleston, Savannah, and Miami ports. He hides them under fake pottery, cleaning supplies, anything that can pass customs without a second glance. My warehouses… they're part of the pipeline. His shops are the cover that launder the money. It's a dirty game, but it works."

Mace's pulse quickened, the weight of the revelation sinking in. His breathing slowed, steady but controlled, as the walls of the room seemed to close in. Every detail sharpened, the flicker of the fluorescent light overhead, the faint hum of air conditioning, the metallic taste of danger in the back of his throat.

"What changed for you?" Preston pressed, the air crackling with anticipation.

Paul's shoulders slumped slightly, and he cast his gaze downward. "He broke the code. My nephew, Jerry, was involved in that mess with your wife, Mace. When she and her friends were attacked… Leo thought Jerry ratted him out after you caught him in New York. He ordered his men to beat him, almost to death. Jerry's my blood. What he did to him… Leo might as well have done to me."

The room fell silent, the gravity of Paul's words lingering in the thick air. He wiped a tear from the corner of his eye, but Mace couldn't allow himself to soften. Not until he had every piece of the puzzle.

"Of course, my client expects immunity for his cooperation," the lawyer interjected, his voice breaking the quiet like a whip.

Paul turned to Mace, his eyes pleading, yet hollow. "Leo wants you and your wife gone. Both of you. You're a threat to everything he's built, and he won't stop until you're out of the picture."

Mace's chest tightened, every muscle in his body bracing against the storm of emotion threatening to crash over him. Gone. The word echoed in his mind like a death knell. He couldn't allow it. He wouldn't.

He straightened his posture, forcing himself to breathe. "Gone?" The word slipped out of his mouth like ice. His eyes darkened as they locked on Paul. "That's not going to happen."

Paul swallowed hard, and Mace saw fear flash across his face. Not for himself, but for what he knew was coming.

The room felt as though it was vibrating, the walls pulsing with the weight of everything at stake. Mace stared at Paul, his heart hammering as he fought to keep his composure. The danger was no longer a vague threat, it was right in front of him. And now, he had to face it head-on.

Chapter Twenty-Two

MACE gripped his phone tighter as they drove through the narrow streets back downtown. He scanned his messages, the dim glow from the screen casting eerie shadows across his face in the backseat. Searching for a message from Carly, his heart thudded a little faster as he read through them.

Enjoyed my lunch with Samara. Delish. Back home. Taking a nap. Followed by another message. *Samara called. There's a movie she wants to see. Heading out soon for a girl's night.*

He frowned, a knot tightening in his stomach. Something was off.

"Odd," he muttered, his thumb hovering over the next message.

Evan glanced over, sensing Mace's shift in energy. "What's odd?"

Mace didn't look up. His brow furrowed deeper as he read the next text. *At the movies. Don't call or text. You know how I feel about people on their phones in the theater.*

He swallowed hard, unease crawling up his spine. "Carly has barely mentioned Samara in passing. Now, all of a sudden, they're hanging out, going to lunch and a movie?"

Evan gave a half-hearted shrug. "Could be nothing. With the baby coming, maybe she just needed some girl time."

Mace wasn't convinced. Carly had her routine, especially when Ariel and Yara weren't around. This didn't feel like her. He stared at the screen, a cold unease settling over him like a fog.

Chris pulled up in front of the office. "I'll park out back if you want to head in now."

Mace nodded absently, his mind still spinning as he and Evan got out of the car. The sharp click of the door echoed unnervingly in the quiet street. Inside the office building, the fluorescent lights buzzed, making the silence feel even heavier.

As they walked through the lobby, Mace glanced toward Andrew's desk. His jacket was draped over the chair, and his computer was still on, the faint hum filling the empty space. But Andrew was nowhere to be seen.

Mace continued to his office, the familiar sight of his desk offering little comfort. His phone buzzed again in his pocket, but he ignored it for the moment, scanning his computer screen. The schedule stared back at him, a ghost of the day that had been completely rearranged. Hours spent with the Feds grilling Paul had shifted everything. But they had what they'd come for—a damning confession that could take down Simeon "Leo" Clarke.

Simeon…

Mace shook his head, remembering Paul's words: Leo's resentment towards Mace's family, his obsession with control, and how he loathed Carly's involvement with the local community.

He leaned back in his chair, staring at the ceiling. Everything seemed to be converging into something darker, more dangerous than he had anticipated. He needed answers. Now.

He pressed the button on his speakerphone. "Andrew?"

"Yes sir," he answered.

"Gather the team. I've got time for one meeting before I head home. Meet me in the conference room."

There was a crackle of static, followed by silence. Mace frowned and stood abruptly. He walked to the conference room, finding only

Evan seated at the table, his fingers tapping rhythmically against the polished wood.

Andrew entered the room a moment later. "The acquisition team's already flown out west to scout properties. The rest left early to beat traffic. They're heading back to New York for the weekend."

Mace felt a sinking feeling in his gut. The office, usually buzzing with activity, was eerily quiet now, like the calm before a storm. "All right, Andrew. Go ahead and call it a day."

Andrew nodded and quickly excused himself.

Evan rose from his chair but paused, sensing something in the air, a dread that made him hesitate. "What's up?"

Mace didn't respond immediately. His phone rang, cutting through the silence. He glanced at the caller ID—Yara.

"Hey, Mace," she said in a rush.

"What's going on?" His voice was sharp, urgent. "Something's different in your voice."

Yara's response was still fast, panicked. "I've been calling Carly all day. She hasn't picked up once. I even left our emergency code—she never ignores that. Ariel hasn't heard from her either. And then… then I get this random text calling me a—"

"Wait," Mace interrupted, tension coiling in his chest. "You're saying Carly ghosted you?"

"Yes! That's not Carly, Mace. Something's wrong."

He placed the call on speaker so Evan could hear. His stomach was knotting tighter with every word Yara spoke. Evan's expression darkened beside him.

Chris entered the room, reading their faces immediately. "What's going on?"

Yara's voice trembled slightly. "I… I hacked into Carly's phone."

Mace blinked. "You *what*?"

"Not the point right now!" she snapped. "I traced her last location. Her phone and car's GPS have been disabled. Both were last tracked to Folly Beach."

"Thanks, Yara. I've got to go." Mace shot up from his chair, his heart hammering. "Folly Beach? Why would she still be there?" Every nerve in his body screamed that something was horribly wrong. He turned to Chris. "Get those coordinates now. We need to move."

Chris was already on his phone, fingers moving at lightning speed as he activated the security team. "I'll cover the condo and check Aunt Nora's place, then head out to the beach."

But Mace shook his head, adrenaline spiking. "No. I'm going out there myself."

"Mace," Chris said firmly, wiping a sheen of sweat from his brow, "what if this is what Leo's people want? What if they call you with demands for Carly's release? You need to stay close to the phone."

Mace's blood pounded in his ears. The thought of Carly in danger, of her being taken… it was too much. His chest tightened painfully as he declared his intent. "I'm not just sitting around waiting."

Chris raised a hand, trying to calm him. "We've got people already moving. Give us thirty minutes."

"Thirty minutes?" Mace's voice growled. He slammed a fist on the table, the sound echoing through the room. His breath came fast, hard. "If something happens to Carly in that time—"

"We won't let it get that far," Chris interjected, locking eyes with him. "But you've got to give us a chance to set this up right."

Mace's phone buzzed again.

Yara's voice came through. "I just spoke to Samara. She didn't meet with Carly today."

That was the final nail. Mace's heart thundered, his mind racing. He stormed toward the door.

"I'll give you thirty minutes, Chris," Mace said, voice thick with restrained fury. "But after that… I'm going to find my wife myself."

The cold weight of dread settled in his gut as he left the room. Time was slipping away, and with every second, Carly was further out of reach.

CHAPTER TWENTY-THREE

CARLY was enveloped in chaos, but alive. Nala lay crumpled on the floor, her leg bleeding, the dark pool seeping into the cracked wooden boards. Her limp body was a silent reminder that Cassidy had crossed a line. Carly heard Cassidy's breath quickened, matching the chaotic madness of the scene.

"What the hell!" Kayla's shrill voice cut through the tension, her eyes wide with disbelief as she backed into the corner. The flickering light overhead made shadows dance across her face, accentuating her terror. "Cassidy, this is too much. Way too much!" Her finger trembled as she pointed toward Nala. "How do we fix this? This wasn't part of the plan."

Cassidy snapped her head toward Kayla, her expression hard, jaw clenched. "Shut up and let me think." She wiped a bead of sweat from her brow with the back of her hand, pacing the small room like a caged animal, the sound of her boots clicking ominously against the floor. "Check on Carly. See if she's still breathing."

Kayla swallowed hard, hesitating before crouching next to Carly, whose body lay in a heap on the cold floor, her face pallid under the dim light. Kayla's fingers trembled as they brushed Carly's neck, searching for a pulse.

"She's alive, but barely," Kayla muttered, standing quickly as if Carly's fragile state was contagious. "The meds are working. She'll be out for good before sunrise." Her voice wavered, eyes darting to the door as if she might bolt.

Carly lay motionless, but her mind raced. *Don't move. Keep your breathing slow.* She clung to the meditation techniques she'd learned, focusing on each sluggish inhale and exhale. They think I'm out of it. Good. Let them think that. Her pulse pounded in her ears, but her body remained limp, the fog of drugs making it harder to keep the panic at bay.

Cassidy turned back to Kayla, her eyes gleaming with a dangerous glint as she tapped the gun against her temple, the metal cold against her skin. "Leo thinks I'm too soft. Told me to just drug her, make her compliant. But this?" She gestured around the room. "This is what happens when a boy tries to plan a woman's work." A twisted smirk pulled at her lips, followed by a low, dark chuckle. "Plan B is in full effect now."

Kayla crossed her arms, her voice shaking with frustration. "And what's that supposed to be? This is way beyond what I signed up for, Cassidy. A little intimidation, sure. But murder?" She shook her head, her eyes narrowing. "I didn't agree to this."

Cassidy shot her a look that could cut glass. "You don't have to agree. You just have to do what I say. Search Nala for Carly's keys. They're probably in her pocket." Her voice was sharp, each word biting through the air with deadly precision. "Move Carly's car, then drive Nala's car away from the beach to throw off anyone looking for her until I figure things out. Leave now, since you want out of here. I'll call you later."

Kayla bit her lip, glancing uneasily at Nala before yanking the keys from her pocket and heading for the door. The sound of the door slamming behind her echoed like a gunshot in the tense silence.

Cassidy looked down at Nala, her breath ragged as blood slowly oozed from the wound in her leg, the stain creeping across the floor.

"I need to stage this," Cassidy muttered, pulling on a pair of gloves. She kicked Nala's gun closer to Nala's body with her foot. "Let's make it look like Carly fought back."

Moving quickly, Cassidy wiped down her own gun with a throw blanket, removing any trace of her fingerprints, then slipped the remaining bullets out of the chamber with practiced ease. She crouched next to Carly's limp body, grabbing her hand and curling her fingers around the gun, her movements rough but efficient.

Carly's pulse fluttered, her body cold and clammy under Cassidy's touch. Cassidy watched as Carly's eyelids fluttered briefly, her eyes rolling back into her head like a lifeless doll.

"You're already half gone," Cassidy whispered, her tone eerily calm. "Won't be long now."

Her phone buzzed, breaking the tense silence. She yanked it from her pocket, glancing at the screen.

"Cass, people at the restaurant are asking questions," a low male voice warned. "The manager is pulling tapes from earlier. They're looking for that rich lady. You need to disappear. Now."

Cassidy placed a hand on her stomach. "Thanks for the heads-up."

She hung up and surveyed the scene one last time. Nala bleeding out, Carly fading fast. She swallowed hard, her gaze fixed on Carly's pregnant belly.

"Sorry, baby," Cassidy muttered, her voice soft, but devoid of emotion. "You didn't deserve this. But there's always collateral damage."

The room seemed to darken as she moved toward the door, each step heavier than the last. With a flip of her wrist, she switched off the lights, casting the room into shadows. Her hand lingered on the doorknob, her lips curling into a bitter smile.

"At least their deaths will be painless," she whispered. "That's the least I can do."

And with that, she slipped out, leaving Carly and Nala in the dark, the silence thick with danger and the weight of what was to come.

Chapter Twenty-Four

MACE'S heart pounded as he gripped the steering wheel, his knuckles white, veins pulsing. The thirty-minute drive from downtown Charleston to Folly Beach felt like hours, each passing second tightening the knot of dread in his gut. The highway stretched endlessly before him, though traffic was sparse. Palm trees bent in the wind, their leaves rustling like whispers of ghosts, while sea grasses along the marsh swayed, mocking his urgency. Normally, the drive brought peace—memories of his grandparents' beach house and the solace it had once provided—but now, it felt like a corridor of uncertainty, pushing him toward something dark.

"No, don't think that," he muttered, shaking his head as he wiped the sweat from his brow.

The thought of losing Carly, of losing their unborn child, was unbearable. He forced his eyes to the road, breathing deeply, trying to clear the fog of panic that threatened to consume him. His phone rang, jarring him from his spiraling thoughts. He hit the answer button on the steering wheel.

"Mace, my guys reviewed the footage from the restaurant," Chris's voice came through, crackling over the Bluetooth. "Carly didn't meet with Samara, but there was trouble with Nala."

"Nala?" Mace's jaw clenched as he swerved onto the narrow road leading to the family beach house. "What kind of trouble?"

"There was a brief exchange of words between Carly and Nala before Nala stormed out of the restaurant. Then, Carly was approached by two women asking her to sign books. One of them hovered over Carly, and her actions were suspicious, but the camera's angle wasn't great. We couldn't see exactly what she was doing."

A chill ran down Mace's spine. "And Carly didn't leave with them?"

"No," Chris replied. "The last ping from her phone was at your beach house. After that, nothing. GPS on her car? Disabled. We're canvassing the area now."

Mace gripped the wheel harder, his pulse racing. The road blurred as he pulled into the driveway of the beach house. He cut the engine and leaned forward, pressing his forehead against the cool leather of the steering wheel. His mind raced, swirling with worst-case scenarios, but he pushed them down. He had to stay sharp. Focused.

Chris's voice was steady, trying to offer some sense of control. "We've already searched the house, Mace. There's nothing there. Go home. We'll find her."

"I can't, Chris. I can't leave until I know for sure." Mace's voice wavered, the desperation he'd tried to keep in check breaking through. "I'll keep calm, but I need to do this. If someone calls or reaches out for a ransom, you'll be the first to know."

"All right," Chris conceded. "Just keep acting like you don't see the team tailing you."

Mace forced a laugh, hollow and bitter. "Easy enough. Bye."

As he stepped out of the car, his phone buzzed again. A message from Ariel: *On my way back to Charleston. Aunt Nora's worried about Carly.*

Mace swallowed the lump in his throat as he made his way to the house. The cool evening air brushed his skin, carrying the salty scent of the ocean. Pebbles crunched beneath his shoes as he moved past the succulent plants lining the walkway. The porch light was on, but the house sat in eerie darkness, casting long shadows across the yard.

He unlocked the door and stepped inside. The air felt thick and heavy. The faint scent of jasmine and vanilla, Carly's favorite, lingered in the room, and it struck him like a punch to the gut. She'd been here. Recently. The soft floral aroma calmed him for a split second before reality crashed back in. He had no idea where she was now.

"Please," he whispered into the stillness, his voice cracking. "Let me find her."

The room looked different. His mother had convinced him to redecorate years ago, but he barely noticed the cool blues and grays that now painted the walls. His eyes scanned the space frantically, searching for anything, any sign. He collapsed onto the couch, fingers digging into his phone, as if answers could somehow appear on the screen.

His phone buzzed again. A message from Emily Anne Bradley. *Sorry to bother you, but you said I could call if I needed help. Can we meet?*

"Not now," he muttered, shoving the phone back into his pocket.

He wandered through the house, checking each room. Nothing. Just as Chris had said, no sign of Carly. His stomach twisted as he made his way back outside, closing the door. He leaned against the porch railing, staring into the darkness. The sound of distant waves crashing against the shore only heightened his frustration.

His phone rang again. His mother's name, Lucille, appeared on the screen. He hesitated, then answered.

"Hey, son." Her voice was soft, maternal, a lifeline to the world he was losing grip on. "Evan told me about Carly. Is it true?"

His silence answered her.

"Mace…" Her voice faltered, laden with worry. "Where are you?"

"I don't know where she is." He rubbed his temple, eyes closing against the rising swell of emotion. "I should've protected her. This is my fault."

"Mace, stop. It's not your fault," she said, her words firm yet gentle. "You can't carry that guilt. Focus on finding her."

"I spent ten years without her. I can't lose her again," Mace whispered, staring at the darkening sky. "She's my everything."

His thumb fumbled over the key fob to Carly's car, the cold metal biting into his skin. He pressed the button absentmindedly.

Beep. Beep.

Mace froze. His eyes snapped to the garage next door, where a dim light blinked behind the shade covering the window. His heart skipped a beat.

"Mom, I have to go," he said, barely hearing her response as he hung up and darted across the yard, toward the garage. His breath came in short, rapid bursts as he reached for the handle, yanking it open.

There, tucked in the shadows, was Carly's car. His pulse quickened as sweat dripped down his face. He had found her. Or at least, he hoped he was close.

Chapter Twenty-Five

A BLACK SUV screeched to a halt at the curb, tires skidding as several men in dark tactical gear spilled out, sprinting after Mace as he tore across the lawn. His breath came in rapid, shallow bursts, heart pounding so hard he could hear it in his ears. Sweat slicked his palms, making his grip on the doorframe slippery as he pounded on the front door.

"Carly!" Mace shouted, voice raw with fear. "Carly!" He banged harder, desperation mounting with every unanswered call. No reply.

He raced to the window, his fingers trembling. Through the small gap in the blinds, his eyes locked on a figure sprawled on the floor, motionless. His stomach churned, a wave of nausea tightening his chest. The metallic scent of blood, faint but unmistakable, seeped through the cracks in the door.

"I think I see a body," he said, his voice shaky as he turned to his security team. "Those shoes—those are Carly's."

His vision tunneled, focusing on her still legs, clad in shoes he knew too well. Panic threatened to paralyze him, but he clenched his jaw, trying to force his way through the window. His fist flew toward the glass, but Chris caught it mid-swing.

"Mace, we've got a battering ram," Chris said, his voice firm. "Let my men handle this."

Impatience clawed at Mace's throat. Every second felt like a lifetime. "We're wasting time!"

The body inside remained still, the room ominously quiet.

Two men returned from scouting the backyard, shaking their heads. "No one's answering back there either," one of them said.

Mace's pulse quickened. *What if we're too late?* His mind spiraled with every dark possibility.

The sound of heavy boots crunching on gravel signaled the arrival of the battering ram.

"Let's move," Chris ordered, his men stepping into position.

The door exploded inward with a deafening crack, wood splintering under the force of the ram. The smell hit Mace first, blood, thick and iron-rich. His stomach turned as he stepped over the threshold, eyes locking on Carly's crumpled form.

"Carly!" His voice cracked as he rushed to her side, falling to his knees beside her. The metallic tang of blood overwhelmed his senses.

But as he got closer, he realized Carly wasn't alone. Nala lay beneath her, blood pooling from a wound in her leg. Carly's hands pressed a throw blanket to Nala's thigh, her body trembling with exhaustion but still conscious. Mace cradled Carly's head, tears streaking down his face as he checked for a pulse.

"She's alive," he breathed, relief washing over him as he felt the faint thrum under his fingers. "Thank God." His shirt clung to him, drenched in sweat, and droplets fell onto Carly's face as she stirred, eyes fluttering open.

"Mace?" she croaked, blinking slowly.

"Who hurt you?" His voice was barely above a whisper, still reeling from the shock.

"It's not me." Carly's voice was hoarse but steady. She took a deep breath, grimacing in pain. "It's Nala. She was shot."

Mace's hand tightened on hers, his throat constricting with the emotions welling inside him. "I thought…" He couldn't finish the sentence.

"Take off your belt," Carly ordered, her voice gaining strength. She winced, gesturing at Nala. "She needs a tourniquet. Now."

Mace blinked, momentarily stunned by Carly's sudden command. "What?"

"Stop the bleeding!" she snapped, glaring at him. "I owe her an ass-kicking later. She needs to live."

Despite the grim situation, a faint smile tugged at the corner of Mace's mouth. Carly's fire, even now, was unquenchable. He quickly removed his belt and tied it tightly around Nala's leg, slowing the flow of blood as the paramedics burst through the door. They worked swiftly, taking over from Mace and Carly.

"We've got her," one said, applying pressure bandages to Nala's wound.

Carly slumped back, exhaustion finally overtaking her as they started an IV on her. Mace's heart skipped as he noticed movement from Carly's belly. The paramedics checked the baby's heartbeat, and Mace exhaled a shaky breath when he heard the strong, steady rhythm.

"We need to get her to the hospital," one of the medics said, urgency clear in his voice.

As they prepared Carly for transport, she turned her head, eyes blazing with fury. "Nala helped some women poison me," she said, her voice filled with venom as she glanced at the unconscious Nala beside her.

Before Mace could react, Chris and the security team marched in with two women, hands cuffed behind their backs. Carly's eyes narrowed into dangerous slits as she recognized them.

"That's them," she spat, her chest heaving with anger. "They tried to kill me and my child."

Chris nodded grimly. "We caught them on the security footage. They were trying to flee the island. We've got them now."

Carly turned toward them and narrowed her eyes. "You need to get what's coming to you." She tried to get off the stretcher but was restrained. Her chest heaved with anger.

"Don't worry, Mrs. Moore. They're not talking now, but they will," Perry assured her. "We've had this one under surveillance for a while."

Chris placed his hand on Cassidy's shoulder, the taller of the two. "She works directly for Simeon Clarke. I'm sure Miss Cassidy Seymour might be loyal, but she's not interested in doing time for her boss."

Cassidy looked over her shoulder at Chris standing behind her.

After Carly was secured on the stretcher, her fury momentarily gave way to exhaustion. Mace gripped her hand, walking alongside her as they wheeled her to the waiting ambulance. His breath was shallow, his mind racing.

"I'm not leaving your side," he promised, his voice hoarse. "Not now. Not ever."

The paramedics nodded, and without another word, they rushed her toward the hospital. Mace remained by her side, the weight of everything pressing down on him like a vise. He had nearly lost her, nearly lost everything. But he wasn't letting go now.

***

It wasn't what they'd expected. Carly and Mace had envisioned this moment for months—the birth of their child, a joyous event surrounded by family, laughter, and the glow of new life. The luxury birthing suite came prepared with every comfort: soft lighting, silky bedding, and soothing music that gently hummed in the background. A peaceful fountain trickled in the corner, casting a calming ambiance. They had toured the suite just weeks before, imagining the joy that would fill it when their baby arrived.

But now, the sterile glare of fluorescent hospital lights replaced their dreamy vision.

"Don't leave me," Carly's voice trembled as the wheels of the gurney clattered along the cold, hard floor, the soft comfort of the birthing suite now a distant memory. She clutched Mace's hand, her grip tight, knuckles white.

"I'm not going anywhere," Mace whispered, his voice hoarse as he bent down to kiss her forehead. Her skin was slick with sweat, her face pale.

"Mr. Moore, the baby is in distress." The doctor's voice cut through the tension like a blade, her expression hidden behind a mask and surgical scrubs. "We need to operate immediately. This is an emergency."

Mace's heart sank. *Emergency*. The word echoed in his mind, hollow and terrifying. The air felt heavy, almost suffocating. Mace kissed her hand, his lips brushing her cool skin, desperate to comfort her when he felt powerless to do so. "I'm right here," he whispered.

Her gaze locked onto his, her eyes wide with fear and pain. She held on to him as though he was her lifeline. Time stretched thin, their breaths synchronized, every second feeling like a countdown. "But the baby isn't due for two more weeks…" Carly's voice faltered, pain tightening her face as the contractions began to seize her. She winced, her free hand gripping her stomach, her breath shallow and fast. "Oh my God… it hurts. Please, Mace, don't leave me," she said, her breath ragged. Fear threaded through her words.

Mace squeezed her hand one last time before the nurse pried his fingers from hers, guiding him back. "I'll be right here waiting," he called, trying to sound strong, but the quiver in his voice betrayed him.

"We'll come out and let you know about your wife and child as soon as we can," the doctor added before the team pushed Carly's gurney through the hospital corridor, the wheels squealing as they sped toward the operating room.

The double doors loomed ahead, tall and foreboding, leading to the operating room.

The doors swung open then shut with a hollow *thud*, separating him from Carly. His chest tightened as if the weight of the entire hospital was pressing down on him. He stared at the doors, helpless, watching the flashing red light above them.

The clock ticked loudly in the silence that followed. Every passing minute stretched his nerves to the breaking point. He could still hear her voice in his head, trembling with fear, and the doctor's words echoed relentlessly: *the baby is in distress.*

Mace's legs felt weak as he paced the empty corridor, his pulse pounding in his ears. His palms were damp, his throat dry. He fought the urge to burst through those doors, to be at Carly's side, but he knew he couldn't. He couldn't do anything but wait.

In the waiting room, the world slowed to a crawl, every sound amplified. The squeak of a gurney being wheeled down the hall, the distant hum of machines, the faint chatter of nurses, and above it all, the deafening thud of his own heartbeat.

Time felt distorted, and with every passing second, the fear that something might go wrong grew heavier in his chest. He imagined the worst—the unbearable possibilities flashing through his mind in vivid detail. What if something happened to Carly? What if they lost the baby?

He clenched his fists, his nails digging into his palms as he fought to keep himself together. He couldn't let his mind go there. Not now.

The seconds dragged on, each one a lifetime. Finally, the door creaked open and the doctor stepped out, her expression masked, unreadable. Mace's heart stopped, his breath frozen in his chest.

"Mr. Moore." she said softly, motioning him forward.

He swallowed hard, bracing for whatever news she was about to deliver. The stress in the air was so thick it was hard to breathe.

"Your wife is fine, and the baby…" the doctor said.

Mace held his breath for what seemed like an eternity.

"You have a healthy daughter," the doctor announced the birth of his child.

CHAPTER TWENTY-SIX

"SHE'S so beautiful." Mace stood next to Carly, hours later, looking through the clear plastic at their daughter in her incubator. She had required additional oxygen and close monitoring of her vital signs.

In the softly lit neonatal intensive care unit, a delicate atmosphere surrounded the incubator where their newborn rested. Her presence radiated a sense of hope for their family. The incubator, a haven of warmth and protection, cradled her like a cocoon, its transparent walls allowing the world to glimpse the precious life within.

Tiny, delicate fingers curled around the edge of a miniature blanket, knitted with care and colored with soft pink hues. Her skin, a canvas of warmth wrapped in a gentle golden brown, reflected the beauty of her Moore and Rivers roots. A crown of soft, dark curls framed her delicate face, promising a future adorned with strength and resilience. Her peaceful slumber was interrupted only by the rhythmic monitoring of electronic equipment. Long dark eyelashes rested gently against her tiny cheeks.

"We have created a precious, beautiful baby girl." Carly smiled. "But I think we're a little biased." She placed her hands through the holes in the plastic and caressed her daughter's back. "Mommy loves you so much, Taryn Avery Moore."

Mace beamed a bright smile at his newborn, then at Carly. "She looks like you."

She tilted her head. "I thought she looks like your niece, Emerson. She was given that name in honor of your middle name, Edmund, right?"

"Yes. It would have been strange to call her Edmund." He laughed, then his smile faded. "Thanks for letting me name her. I've always liked the name Taryn, and your research assignment here into local neighborhoods in Charleston at the Avery Institute is what caused our reunion after so many years." He hugged her tightly.

She looked up as a tear rolled down his cheek. They remained close to each other, admiring the new life they had created.

"I couldn't have imagined that this past year would have been the happiest year of my life. I have a wife, and now we're blessed with a wonderful, healthy daughter."

"Sorry for the interruption." The pediatrician approached them. It had been two days since Taryn's birth and the first day she had not had tubes connected to her body. "I have good news. Your baby has been breathing well on her own. She'll be transferred to the regular newborn unit. By tomorrow, we think it will be fine for her to stay in the room with you, Carly."

She opened her mouth wide and covered it with her hands. "That's fantastic news." She let out a breath of relief and smiled. "Now, can you convince my husband to go home and get some rest tonight? He's been camping out at the hospital since I was wheeled in. I think a long shower and a good meal will do him some good."

"Doctor's orders, Mason." He repositioned his stethoscope around his neck. "We're out of the woods for now. Your family will be fine while you get the rest you need. Her obstetrician informed me that Carly's blood pressure is no longer elevated. Her vitals have been stable for the last twenty-four hours, and there's no evidence of the substance used to drug her in her system."

"I could use a shave and a shower." He rubbed the stubble on his chin, then turned to look at Carly. "I'll take you back to your room and then go home."

"Sounds like a great plan." The doctor extended his hand to Mace and to Carly. "You have a gorgeous baby girl." He checked the information on the monitors before he departed.

"Call me when you find out that they're transferring Taryn to your room. Do you need anything? I'll bring it when I come." Mace placed his hand around her shoulder and walked toward the door.

"I just need to know that you're getting some rest," she reassured him.

He placed a hand to his mouth to stifle a yawn. "I'll return a call from Evan. He had some info from Preston. Then I'll get some rest."

***

"When is Mace coming?" Yara asked on the three-way call with Carly and Ariel.

"I called to tell him they were bringing Taryn to the room earlier than they had planned," Carly replied. "He said he was on his way, but that was over an hour ago. He probably fell asleep after our call. He had been up for most of the last two days. I know he's tired." She bit her lip and looked at the clock. "Aunt Nora and Mace's mother stopped by and stayed for a wonderful visit."

She looked at her daughter swaddled in her blanket, resting quietly in her arms. Taryn let out a sweet whimper before settling back into slumber.

"Was that Taryn?" Ariel asked. "Do you need to do something for her? We can call back later."

Carly placed the phone that was on speaker on the bed and wrapped Taryn in her arms, closer to her exposed chest, allowing them skin to skin contact. "She's fine. Baby girl has been fed and changed." Her voice was melodic and calming as she took in a large whiff of her daughter's intoxicating newborn smell. "Let's stick with the plan for the two of you to stop by later today."

"We'll call to make sure it's after a diaper change," Yara commented with laughter.

"What?" Carly responded, her mood playful. "I wouldn't consider letting the two of you miss out on the fragrant smell of brown baby mush wrapped in pixie dust and warmed with sunshine."

"Ariel, I think our friend has lost her mind. She's gone ga-ga for that baby."

"I think I might try my hand at a diaper change. Yara, get used to it. That's what aunties do," Ariel told her.

Carly's phone buzzed with a message. "I think that's a message from Mace. I'd better check it. I'll see the two of you later today. Bye."

She frowned as she looked at the message.

I've been delayed. I'll tell you about it when I get there. We need to talk.

Chapter Twenty-Seven

MACE had been on his way to the hospital when Emily Anne Bradley called him that morning. She left several messages, each with more urgent demands for a meeting with him today.

"The road to hell is often paved with good intentions," he recalled before answering her message.

They met on the hospital grounds in one of its gardens.

"I know this isn't the best time to ask for a favor, but I had no choice." She made quick, furtive glances around the garden as if suspecting someone may be lurking in the bushes. Her arms were filled with something in a light pink baby blanket. "Congratulations on the birth of your daughter."

"Thank you." Mace furrowed his brow, curious about the contents in her arm.

He made a quick assessment that she no longer had a swollen belly. Her clothes were disheveled as if she had gotten dressed in a hurry. Her hair was pulled back in a tight bun, and her eyes were wide like a frightened doe in a battle for her life.

She moved closer to him and spoke in whispered tones. "Your brother has been a godsend to me. He's been helping me get out of the mess I'm in, but I couldn't ask him to do this for me. He already has four children, and I don't know his wife." She moved even closer to him. They were almost toe to toe.

He took a breath to center himself and rubbed his chin. "I don't understand what this has to do with me. You don't know me or my wife."

She looked around again, her head jerking from one corner of the garden to another. "It's what I feel that is leading me to you. I feel you're a good man. Who else would come knowing I was going to ask for a favor? You came, not one of your assistants. It was through divine intervention that I met your wife. She seemed so happy that you two were going to bring life into the world. Take this." She reached into her large purse on her shoulder and pulled out a baby sling.

Mace took the durable cloth baby carrier, taking a moment to digest what he knew she was about to ask.

She pulled a series of papers out of her bag. "These papers have been notarized. It gives you temporary custody of my baby until I can get back to her. I also included her discharge papers from the hospital. She's healthy."

She handed him the papers that had his name on them as the agent to receive custody of a baby named Talia.

"Talia Liliana Bradley is her name." He perused the paperwork quickly before looking at her. "Let me offer you and Talia a safe place to stay while you sort things out. I appreciate the trust you've placed in me to care for your precious girl, but..."

Emily interrupted him, tears streaming down her face. "This is the hardest thing I've ever done in my life. My baby was born two days ago, earlier than expected after her father grabbed me and demanded that I leave with him. Talia saved my life by breaking her waters. He panicked when he saw I was in labor. She saved my life, and now I must save hers. She's not safe with me right now. You've got to help me. I don't have anyone else."

Something stirred in the bushes, making her flinch and almost drop the baby. Mace jumped into action and grabbed her just as Emily Anne was pushing the infant into his arms.

"I promise I'll come back for her as soon as I can." She turned back momentarily before running in the opposite direction. "Tell her how much I love her."

Flinging the bag on her shoulder at his feet, she ran away before Mace could convince her to stay.

He pushed back the folds of the blanket and looked at the innocent little girl as she stirred and opened her soft brown eyes, revealing the soul of a small survivor.

"We'll keep you safe." He looked at the cloudy blue sky, hoping in its vast infinite space, there was an answer to this current dilemma. "I'm not sure how I'm going to explain this to Carly… or Evan for that matter."

A light misty rain fell. He hurried and bent down to pick up the bag.

"First challenge. How do I get a newborn past hospital security?" he wondered out loud.

Mace's heart pounded as he stood outside the hospital entrance, cradling the tiny bundle against his chest. He felt the rapid rise and fall of Talia's soft breaths beneath his hand, her small body tucked securely into the sling. The weight of his decision pressed down on him with each step he took toward the doors. The promise he had made to Emily echoed in his mind, but doubt gnawed at him. *Could he really do this? Could he keep Talia safe?*

He pulled his jacket tighter around the sling, slipping one arm out of the sleeve, as though it were injured. His heart raced, and a slick of sweat dampened his palms despite the cool air. Every step felt like a gamble. He had to get upstairs to talk to Carly, but without drawing attention, without anyone noticing the precious cargo hidden beneath his coat.

"I need you to stay quiet until we get upstairs," he whispered to Talia, though the newborn didn't understand. Her soft, barely audible whimper was her only response.

Mace pushed open the heavy glass doors, stepping into the bustling hospital corridor. The bright fluorescent lights buzzed faintly, and the smell of antiseptic hit him like a wave. The air was thick with the noise of people talking and staff rushing by—everything seemed louder than usual, his nerves amplifying each sound.

He kept his eyes forward, focused, and moved with purpose toward the bank of elevators at the far end of the hall. His stomach twisted into tight knots with every stride, and he had to force himself to maintain a calm pace, even though his instinct screamed at him to run.

The doors to the elevator slid open as he approached, and for a moment, relief flooded through him. It was empty. No eyes on him. He stepped inside quickly and hit the button for Carly's floor, his fingers cool as they brushed the controls. But as the doors began to close, a foot slipped between them, forcing them open again.

Mace's pulse skyrocketed, and he sucked in a sharp breath, freezing as three nurses in scrubs and a man in a suit entered the car. His throat tightened as they stepped in, their chatter filling the small space. He plastered on a tight smile, shifting slightly to the corner, hoping to blend into the background.

One of the nurses turned her head, her eyes locking onto his sling-covered arm. She smiled.

"Broken arm?" she asked, her voice light, but her gaze lingered a beat too long.

Mace felt his chest constrict. He opened his mouth, but his mind scrambled for a response as the elevator jolted to a sudden stop, the force of it causing Talia to let out a soft noise—a tiny, almost imperceptible whimper that sent his heart into his throat.

He cleared his throat, shifting his weight to try to mask the sound. "Uh, yeah. Sports injury. Still hurts like hell." He grimaced, pretending to rub his supposedly injured arm that was pressed firmly against the baby's body, comforting her.

The nurse gave him a sympathetic nod, her attention thankfully drifting back to her colleagues as they prepared to exit. "Take care," she called over her shoulder as they stepped out of the elevator.

Mace exhaled, the tension in his shoulders easing slightly as the doors slid shut behind them. He glanced down at Talia through the small opening in his jacket.

"Good girl," he whispered, his voice barely audible as the elevator resumed its ascent. But his relief was short-lived. He was only halfway through this precarious ordeal. "*Second issue. How do I convince Carly, who just gave birth, to take on a second infant?*"

His stomach churned. How would Carly react? He didn't know. She'd just been through the emotional trauma of an attack and the physical toll of giving birth. Her body and mind were already stretched to their limits. And now he was about to drop this on her—a baby she wasn't expecting.

***

Carly gingerly placed Taryn in the bassinet after her feeding, her body still recovering from giving birth. As she looked at her daughter, a pang of unease crept into her chest. This moment was supposed to be perfect—the room she had dreamed about, with soft lighting, a peaceful ambiance, and the comforting hum of life surrounding her. Instead, their first moments together had been in the sterile, cold environments of the operating room and the neonatal ICU. The steady beeping of machines still echoed in her ears, reminding her of the fragility of it all. Taryn's arrival hadn't been the joyous, smooth event she had envisioned.

Mace pushed open the door to the suite, his entrance abrupt, slicing through Carly's lingering reflections. "The nursery on this floor is full," he said, a strange edge to his voice. "Do you know how many babies were born on the same day as Taryn?" His words tumbled out too quickly, betraying an undercurrent of something she couldn't quite place.

"No idea," Carly muttered, her eyes narrowing as she noticed his arm in a sling. "What happened to you?" She stepped closer, her gaze shifting from his face to the jacket hanging oddly from his body. "Why is your arm in a sling?"

Mace moved quickly, placing a finger to his lips, urging her to lower her voice. Something was off. He closed the door with a soft click, his movements calculated, deliberate. Carly's pulse quickened. What was he hiding? Before she could press further, Mace pulled the jacket apart, revealing the unexpected.

Her breath caught in her throat as she saw the tiny infant nestled beneath his coat. Carly's jaw dropped, her voice barely a whisper. "What have you done?" She pointed at the baby, who whimpered, her small fists writhing in discomfort.

"I think she's hungry," Mace said, his voice soft but strained. His eyes met hers, a mixture of desperation and pleading swirling in their depths.

Carly's mind reeled, trying to grasp the enormity of the situation. She threw the jacket across the room, speechless. The baby in Mace's arms—how was this even possible? Her brain buzzed with a thousand questions, none of which she could fully articulate. *Who was this child? Why was Mace carrying her?*

"Can you take her?" Mace asked quietly. "I'll explain everything. I promise."

Carly's body moved on autopilot as she reached for the baby, cradling her with instinctive care. The infant felt so small and fragile in her arms.

"I don't know where to start with the questions." Carly's voice cracked as she walked slowly around the room, her thoughts a jumbled mess. She glanced at the baby's face, so innocent and unaware of the turmoil swirling around her. "Where are her parents?" She stopped to meet Mace's eyes. "What's her name? How old is she?"

"Talia," Mace said, rubbing his forehead, clearly struggling with the weight of the situation. "She's two days old. Same as Taryn."

Carly's heart clenched. Two days old. The same age as Taryn. Her gaze bounced between the two girls, the daughter she had carried and this new life thrust into her care.

"How did you get her up here past security?" she asked, her voice sharper now, though Talia's whimpering interrupted her thoughts.

Carly's heart softened as she looked at Talia. Something stirred deep inside her, a wave of empathy, of compassion. She couldn't ignore the baby's need. Moving to her bed, Carly carefully positioned herself with Talia nestled close, creating a soft nest of pillows around them. As her fingers traced Talia's delicate features, she marveled at the similarities. There was an undeniable connection, but confusion clouded her feelings. This wasn't her child. This baby belonged to another woman, another family. Yet as Talia nuzzled against her, seeking comfort, Carly felt a strange bond forming, something intimate and inexplicable.

Mace jumped into action, heading to the fridge to retrieve a bottle of milk. "I'll warm it," he added, glancing at their daughter, who stirred in her bassinet. Carly could see the tension in his shoulders, the weight of his choices hanging heavily over him.

As Carly fed Talia, the room quieted, a hush falling over them. She watched Mace hold Taryn, the scene so peaceful on the surface but roiling with unspoken tension beneath. Mace settled on the bed beside her, his long legs stretching out as he held Taryn close.

"There's something sacred about this," Mace said after a long silence, his voice thick with emotion as he looked at Carly and the two babies.

Carly blinked, her emotions too tangled to speak. She nodded, feeling the lump in her throat grow as she held Talia, the sensation of feeding another woman's child both surreal and deeply intimate.

"This is… interesting," she whispered, her voice soft.

The room shifted, the weight of what they were doing settling into the space around them. After Mace changed Taryn's diaper, Carly placed Talia next to her in the bassinet. Both girls stirred, their tiny hands seeking each other. Carly's breath hitched as the infants' fingers intertwined, gripping tightly as though they had always known one another.

Mace's eyes widened, his voice low and full of awe. "At first, I didn't know how to tell you what happened to me this morning… but our girls… they've helped me find the words."

Our girls.

Carly froze, her heart thudding. She didn't challenge his words, but a deep unease settled in her bones. Talia was a stranger, but there was something undeniable about the connection between them all. For the next hour, he told Carly about his encounter with Emily Anne and Talia.

CHAPTER TWENTY-EIGHT

"HOW did you explain needing two bassinets?" Yara asked, cradling Talia.

Ariel held Taryn snugly against her chest, rocking slowly. Both babies rested, unaware of the strain thickening in the room.

Carly tried to smile, but it felt brittle. "You know Mace." She sighed. "He always finds a way. He had his security guys smuggle in the extra equipment and assemble it right here in the suite." She pointed toward the adjoining room. "We keep one of the bassinets hidden behind the curtain. I tell the nurses Mace is sleeping in there, and so far, Talia's been quiet when anyone comes in."

Ariel raised a skeptical brow. "What's the plan when it's time to check out? You can't exactly leave with two babies when you've only given birth to one."

Carly exhaled shakily, pressing her palms to her eyes. The weight of the situation felt suffocating. "Mace is meeting Evan right now to figure out the legal side of this. Talia's mother, Emily Anne, signed temporary custody papers, asking us to take care of her. But..."

"But it's complicated," Ariel finished, her voice soft but steady as she shifted Taryn's body, gently patting the sleepy infant's back. "There's no way around it, Carly. Even if her mother agreed, Talia's father has rights. It won't be easy."

Yara frowned deeply, shaking her head. "This poor little baby is caught in a mess," she murmured, adjusting Talia's small body over her shoulder.

The room was silent, save for the quiet, rhythmic breathing of the babies and the distant hum of hospital machinery. The lull of the hospital, usually comforting, felt suffocating now, like the quiet before a storm.

Yara glanced at Carly, her expression serious. "Can we have a little real talk?"

"Of course," Carly replied, though she braced herself. She knew where this conversation was heading. Her heart pounded, unsure if she was ready to face it.

Yara gave Ariel a nod, and together they placed the babies down, careful not to disturb their peaceful slumber. The soft rustling of the blankets was the only sound, and for a brief moment, the room was still.

Yara turned back to Carly, crossing her arms, looking between Carly and Ariel. "You told us that Mace has this thing for damsels in distress. I think you're right. He's got it bad if he thinks this is a good idea. I mean really." She crossed her arms. "Has he really thought through what he's asking of you? Are you ready for this? To take care of another baby when you just had Taryn?"

The questions sliced through Carly's already fragile composure. She leaned her head back on the pillow, exhaustion creeping into her bones. "We didn't plan this," she whispered, her voice breaking. "Emily Anne just… handed Talia to Mace and ran off. There was no time to think. And now—"

"Now you're left to deal with the aftermath," Ariel finished, her voice tinged with sympathy. "I know you trust Mace, but you can't tell me this doesn't feel… off."

Carly's breath hitched. She tightened her grip on the sheets, the fabric rough against her skin, grounding her in the chaos. "I believe him," she said, her voice firmer than she felt. "He's never lied to me."

Ariel and Yara exchanged a look but said nothing. The silence was louder than any words they could have spoken, the air thick with doubt and unspoken fears.

Carly sat up, running her fingers through her hair, the weight of her damp curls heavy against her scalp. She needed a break, even if it was just for a few minutes. Her body ached for a moment of solitude, something to help her think clearly in this swirling mess.

"Can you watch the girls while I take a quick shower?" Carly asked, pushing herself off the bed.

"You need it," Ariel said, wrinkling her nose playfully. "We've got the girls."

Yara helped Carly to her feet, nudging her toward the bathroom. "Take your time. We'll handle things here."

The warm water cascading over Carly's skin felt like a lifeline. For a moment, she allowed herself to breathe, the noise of the hospital, the pressure of the situation, all fading into the background. But as the steam filled the room, her thoughts refused to settle. The shower wasn't long enough to wash away the dread tightening her chest.

When she emerged, wrapped in a robe, her hair still damp and tangled from the shower, Carly sensed something was wrong. The room felt too still. Too tense.

She glanced at the bassinets, her heart stuttering. Taryn lay peacefully, her tiny body curled in a blanket, the hospital band marked "Baby Moore" still securely wrapped around her arm. But where—

"Where's Talia?" Carly's voice came out sharper than intended, panic rising. Her eyes shifted from Ariel to Yara, who stood frozen, guilt and fear written across their faces.

"We tried to stop it," Yara said, her voice trembling. "The bathroom door locked behind you. We knocked, but you didn't hear us over the piped in music, the water running, and your singing."

Carly's breath quickened. "What happened?"

"A nurse came in," Ariel continued, her face pale. "She said you hit the call bell, probably by mistake. She came in and offered to help with the baby. Before we knew it, she… she took Talia."

"She what?" Carly's voice cracked as she rushed to the empty bassinet, her fingers gripping the edge.

"Her badge said she was Nurse Connie," Yara whispered, her voice barely audible. "She had all the right credentials. I thought—"

"Connie Hudson?" Carly interrupted, her heart hammering. "She's new. She thinks she has Taryn."

The room seemed to close around her. The walls felt as though they were caving in, the air too thin. Carly could barely think as her mind raced, trying to grasp what had happened. Talia was gone. Her throat tightened, and she instinctively reached for Taryn, pulling the infant into her arms. The baby stirred, her little fingers curling against Carly's chest.

Ariel was already on the phone. "Mace is still with Evan. I'm going to join them now to figure out what we can do."

Carly barely heard her, her thoughts spiraling. *How had she let this happen? How had everything slipped out of her control so quickly?*

Yara wrapped her arms around Carly's shoulders, her voice soft but urgent. "We'll get her back, Carly. We'll figure this out."

Carly could only nod, though her mind was screaming with doubt. She held Taryn tighter, feeling the baby's heartbeat against her chest, but the hole Talia left behind was already gaping, a void that seemed impossible to fill.

"Say something." Yara's voice cracked as she spoke, her tear-streaked face pleading for a response. "You can curse me out or tell me off, just say *something*. I can't stand the silence."

Carly barely heard her as she threw on casual clothes. After dressing, Carly sat down, rocking slowly in the white chair beside Taryn's bassinet. The rhythmic creaking was the only sound in the room. She glanced at Taryn, still sleeping peacefully, oblivious to the turmoil swirling around her mother. The soft rise and fall of the baby's chest was a painful contrast to Carly's erratic breathing.

Her phone buzzed, breaking through her thoughts. She picked it up, reading the message on the screen.

"It's Mace," she said quietly, her voice flat. "He says we'll handle this together after he finishes discussing options with Evan."

She turned her gaze back toward the window, staring blankly at the view of the Ashley River, the water glinting in the late afternoon sun as if nothing in the world had gone wrong. The calmness of the scene felt almost mocking, a far cry from the chaos she felt inside.

Yara shifted uncomfortably. "I know you're mad at me. Just say it. If you blame me, tell me."

Carly shook her head slowly. "I don't blame you." Her voice was soft, almost distant, as if she were talking to herself more than Yara. "My silence isn't about you. I'm just… processing everything." The words felt inadequate, as though they couldn't hold the weight of what was truly happening.

Yara came across the room, pulling a chair close to Carly's rocker until their knees were almost touching. The proximity made the air between them feel heavy, full of things unsaid, the tension palpable.

"Will you share what you're thinking?" Yara asked gently.

Carly hesitated, her eyes fixated on Taryn, the only thing grounding her in that moment. "When Mace brought Talia here… I didn't know how to feel. It was like—" She stopped rocking, holding her hands up as if to catch the thought in midair. "No, I *did* know. I didn't want another child. I wanted to focus on Taryn. I wanted to give her all of me." Her voice trembled, betraying the strength she tried to project.

"I get that." Yara nodded, her face still lined with worry.

Carly let out a shaky breath, her gaze locked on Taryn's sleeping form. "But something happened," she whispered, more to herself than Yara. "When I held them both, Taryn and Talia… it was like my heart just… expanded. Like I could hold them both, love them both. And for the first time, I wanted to. I *wanted* to take care of her." She swallowed hard, her throat tight as tears welled up. She lowered her head, trying to hide the emotions that were threatening to break free. "I decided to open my heart to that little girl, and she was taken away from me."

The sound of her own words hit Carly like a punch to the gut. Her chest tightened, the ache nearly unbearable as she tried to breathe through the wave of helplessness. The quiet weight of the room pressed down on her, amplifying the emptiness left by Talia's absence.

"I don't feel like a stranger to her," Carly murmured, her voice cracking under the weight of her emotions. "For some reason, her mother chose us, *me* and Mace, to take care of her. She trusted us. And I… I feel like I need to honor that, to keep her safe. But now…" Her words faltered, caught in the uncertainty that had plagued her since Talia was taken. She rubbed her temples, the pressure in her head building with every conflicting thought.

Outside, the world went on—birds chirped, the river shimmered, cars passed. But inside the room, Carly felt frozen, teetering on the edge of something she couldn't control. The suspense of not knowing what would come next gnawed at her, making every second feel like an eternity.

"I don't know what to do," she finally admitted, her voice barely audible.

The admission hung in the air, fragile and raw. She felt Yara's presence beside her, felt the warmth of her hand gently resting on her knee, but it didn't ease the conflict raging inside her.

"We'll figure it out," Yara said softly, though Carly heard the uncertainty in her voice too.

Carly squeezed her eyes shut, trying to summon the strength she needed to believe that. To believe they could fix this. But with every second that ticked by, the uncertainty gnawed at her. The image of Talia's empty bassinet haunted her, a painful reminder of how easily things could slip from her grasp.

***

"Bruh, you're telling me you didn't know Emily Anne before you met her in my office?" Evan's voice was sharp, his eyes narrowing as he looked at Mace over the top of his glasses. He lowered his head to continue scanning the papers Mace had handed him from Emily Anne. "I'm her lawyer. Why didn't she talk to me about this?"

Mace stopped pacing, his movements halting as though he'd run into a wall. He glanced over his shoulder, frustration simmering beneath the surface. "I could ask you the same damn thing. She's your client, so why *didn't she* discuss this with you?" He turned to fully face Evan, the weight of the situation pressing on him. "For a minute, I thought—" He hesitated, the words hanging precariously on his tongue.

Evan's eyes flared with warning as he threw his glasses onto the pile of documents in front of him. "Don't even go there. You weren't about to accuse me of being Talia's father, were you?" His jaw tightened, and the conflict between the brothers seemed to thicken the air around them.

Mace shrugged, trying to keep his voice steady, though doubt gnawed at him. "You're a man, she's an attractive woman. Things happen. But like I said, that thought only crossed my mind for a minute." He nodded toward the folder Evan hadn't yet opened. "I had my investigative team run a test. She's not a Moore." His voice wavered slightly as he pointed at the papers with information about Talia, his uncertainty now battling with the facts. "I don't know why she gave the baby to me. Emily said she thought Carly was nice and would take care of her."

Evan leaned back in his chair, his gaze piercing. "You know that's asking a lot of your wife." He absentmindedly chewed on the end of his glasses, the gears in his mind visibly turning. "So, Carly's willing to do this? To care for Talia at least temporarily so she doesn't end up in the system?"

Mace nodded, but the movement felt heavier than it should have. "Yes. Carly's agreed. We can't let Talia suffer because of this mess. She's innocent."

He resumed pacing, the rhythmic tap of his shoes against the hardwood matching the chaotic beat of his heart. His mind raced, torn between protecting his family and honoring the trust Emily had placed in him.

"What do you know about Emily's family?" Mace asked, desperation lacing his words.

"Not much," Evan said, crossing his legs at the ankles as he leaned back in his chair, a faint creak breaking the silence. "Her parents are dead. She was estranged from her husband. He didn't want kids. It was one of the reasons she left him. She said he had a temper. Blamed her for getting pregnant. I took her case pro bono to help with the divorce." He glanced out the window, as if searching for some answer in the skyline. "She said she planned to keep the baby."

Mace's stomach churned as he resumed pacing, the tension coiling tighter around him with every passing second. "What are the chances of us getting temporary custody?"

"The baby isn't related to you." Evan sighed. "Even with this paperwork, we'll have to take it to court."

A knock at the door interrupted them, pulling their attention. Ariel stepped inside, her face a mixture of determination and concern.

"Hey, guys," she greeted, dropping her bag on the table. "You said you were in the executive wing of the hospital. Do you know how many meeting rooms are here?" She pulled out a chair, her frown deepening as she sat. "I didn't want to share this over the phone, but… we have a problem."

Evan's phone rang with a sharp, fire-alarm sound, making everyone in the room tense. "Hold on," he said, raising a finger. "This is Laura, my assistant. We only use this line for emergencies." He answered quickly, his expression shifting as he spoke. "What's going on?"

Mace stopped pacing and stood by Evan, his heart pounding harder.

Evan's face paled as Laura spoke. He fumbled for the speakerphone button. "Repeat that. My brother and Attorney Ariel Dennison are here."

Laura's voice filled the room, somber and shaky. "I just spoke with Emily's cousin, Sherri Sanders. Emily left with her husband a day ago."

Mace felt his chest tighten, a mix of concern and disbelief taking hold. "She was estranged from her husband," Mace muttered, leaning in closer to the speaker, as if the proximity would change the horrible truth.

"She was," Laura confirmed. "But he convinced her to meet. I warned her to be cautious, but she believed things wouldn't get ugly if they talked."

Mace rubbed his forehead, trying to contain the rising panic. "Did Sherri say anything about the baby?" His voice was barely above a whisper, the weight of the situation crashing down on him.

"She said the baby wasn't with Emily. She doesn't know where Emily took her. Sherri didn't want her going into the foster system, but she can't take care of her either. She's elderly, unwell. Emily… she was trying to figure things out, but…" Laura's voice cracked, her emotion spilling through the line. "Emily was kind. She loved and planned to raise her baby. She wanted the best for her."

Evan sighed, shaking his head. "I'll need her full file. Mace has the baby and he's assuming temporary custody."

Laura's voice lightened with the news. "Right away. Emily kept up with the news reports of Mr. Mace's marriage to Ms. Carly. She also followed the hashtag Mason loves Carly on social media. She told me it was the only bright spot in her day. Despite the pain in her own life, she still believed in fairy tale love stories. You should get the files in the next few minutes. Goodbye." Laura hung up.

Mace's phone buzzed, but he barely noticed it. The room felt too small, the air too thick. He felt Ariel's gaze on him, her eyes full of empathy, but it did nothing to ease the tightening in his chest.

Ariel spoke softly, her voice trembling with emotion. "That poor little girl… She's probably with hospital staff, and they don't even realize she's not Taryn."

Mace's head snapped up, a sudden jolt of adrenaline shooting through him. "Why isn't she with Carly?"

Ariel grimaced. "That's what I came here to tell you. A nurse came and took her, thinking she was your baby. They're going to realize soon enough that she's not."

Mace's heart pounded in his ears as he yanked his phone out of his pocket. His fingers trembled as he typed a second message to Carly. "I'm letting her know I'm on the way."

His mind raced, torn between wanting to protect Carly and their family and the overwhelming responsibility Emily Anne had thrust upon him. The uncertainty gnawed at him, and for the first time in his life, he felt utterly powerless.

***

Carly's heart raced as she turned to face the door. Mace stepped in, followed closely by Evan and Ariel, their faces grim, the tension thick enough to slice through. Her gaze landed on Mace first. He looked exhausted, the dark circles under his eyes standing out like bruises, as if the weight of the morning had taken a visible toll. The heaviness of it mirrored in the air between them, making her stomach tighten.

As Mace wrapped his arms around her, Carly felt his exhaustion through the rigid set of his shoulders. He offered Yara a grateful nod, his hand resting on her shoulder briefly. The words he spoke were for Yara, something about Preston and the Sindells, but Carly's mind barely registered them. The way Mace's hand trembled slightly against her back set off alarms, stirring a knot of anxiety deep in her chest.

"I'll explain it all to you later," he murmured, turning his tired gaze to Carly. He glanced at her, his hand brushing a strand of hair away from her face. "You okay?"

She nodded, but it was a hollow gesture. Was she okay? The truth was, she didn't know. She hadn't been okay for the past few days. Carly's throat tightened, her thoughts swirling in a haze of trauma.

Mace leaned back, studying her face before his gaze softened. "Do you mind if I hold Taryn for a second?" His voice cracked, the vulnerability breaking through. "I need both of you right now."

Without speaking, Carly stepped aside, watching as Mace scooped their daughter into his arms. Mace held them both close, his breath hitching as he whispered something too quiet for Carly to hear. The baby's soft coos quickly turned into squirming discomfort before a small splatter of vomit stained Mace's shirt. Carly reacted with instinct, handing him a baby wipe, but her mind was elsewhere, clouded by an unease she couldn't shake.

"I've got her," she said quietly, taking Taryn and heading to the bathroom to clean her up. She could hear voices in the other room, but the pounding in her ears made it hard to focus.

Inside the bathroom, she changed Taryn quickly, her hands moving with practiced ease, but her mind was a whirlwind. Why did everything feel as though it was slipping from her grasp? Taryn was hers, that much she was sure of, but Talia, that sweet girl, what was she to them?

Suddenly, the low murmur of conversation from the other room broke into sharp clarity. The sound of several footsteps and the introduction of voices unfamiliar and formal. Carly's pulse quickened, and she carefully leaned her head out from behind the curtain, watching as a group of executives—stiff, formal, grim-faced—entered the room.

Carly heard a voice, formal and rehearsed. "Mr. Moore, I'm the CEO of the hospital and I'm accompanied by members of my executive team. We're here to address the issue of your missing child."

Carly's stomach clenched, and she held Taryn tighter against her chest, her fingers curling instinctively. She wasn't ready for this confrontation, not now.

"We take baby abductions very seriously," the CEO continued, his words clipped and precise. "The baby that was returned to the nursery wasn't wearing a security bracelet, and upon investigation, we discovered she wasn't your child."

Carly could feel Mace's posture stiffen, even from the bathroom. His calm, professional exterior never faltered, but she knew him too well. Underneath the surface, he was boiling. She wished she could say something, do something, to make this all go away. But what could she do? She felt powerless, her daughter in her arms and another child she wasn't sure she should claim tugging at her heart.

Carly's pulse quickened as the low murmur of voices drifted throughout the room.

Carly peeked around the doorframe. The group of men and women, all dressed in severe, dark suits, stood near the doorway. Their expressions remained somber, their presence heavy, as though they were here to deliver news no one wanted to hear. Carly's throat tightened as she caught sight of Nurse Connie, her eyes swollen from crying. It only confirmed Carly's growing dread that something was terribly wrong.

What were they going to say?

She forced herself to breathe, turning her attention back to Taryn. The sleeper's soft fabric felt foreign in her hands, slippery under the pressure of her frayed nerves. The cold air from the nearby vent brushed across Carly's skin, sending a shiver down her spine. But it wasn't the cold that made her shiver. It was the uncertainty, the fear that gripped her chest like a vise.

She peeped at Mace, standing so still, his face unreadable. *He's holding it together, but for how long?* She knew him too well. Behind that calm exterior, he was just as unsettled as she was. His jaw clenched. His eyes narrowed. Those were the only signs she needed.

The CEO's voice cut through her haze, every word like a punch to the gut. "I can assure you that finding your baby is my top priority. Your family has been a generous benefactor to our hospital."

Our baby. Carly's heart hammered against her ribs, a cold sweat breaking out on the back of her neck. The mention of baby abductions made her head spin. *Please, not Talia.* She blinked hard, her vision blurring for a second as a wave of nausea rolled over her. Was this real? Was this nightmare unfolding around her?

Mace stood with hands clasped behind his back. Evan and Ariel flanked him, stone-faced and silent, ready to act. But Carly felt as if she was drifting in a fog, each new revelation pushing her further from the certainty she so desperately needed.

"The baby that was taken back to the nursery by Nurse Connie didn't have your or your wife's blood type," the CEO continued.

Carly's hands froze mid-motion, her breath catching in her throat. *Not his blood type.* The information registered in her mind. She looked at Taryn, her heart squeezing painfully in her chest. She gently brushed her finger along her daughter's soft cheek, grounding herself for a moment, but the anxiety still swelled within her, unrelenting.

"The good news," the head of security said, stepping forward, "is that no baby has left this floor."

Good news? It felt like a cruel joke. How could there be good news in this suffocating cloud of fear? Carly swallowed hard, her throat dry, her mind racing with a million questions she wasn't sure she wanted the answers to. She heard Evan speaking, calm and collected as ever, but Carly's focus was elsewhere. Her eyes flicked to Yara, who stood by the door, her eyes filled with concern but unwavering. Carly tried to draw strength from her best friend, but the weight of the situation pressed down too heavily.

Carly's body felt stiff as she listened to Nurse Connie's shaky voice. "Mrs. Moore was in the bathroom, and I only wanted to give her and all my patients the best care possible."

The words felt like noise. Carly's mind buzzed with too many emotions at once—fear, disbelief, anger—but above all, uncertainty. *Where is Talia?* She wanted answers. No, she needed answers.

"Where's the child now?" Evan's voice was sharp, cutting through the tension.

Carly bit her lip, her anxiety bubbling to the surface as she rocked Taryn gently in her arms. She forced herself to focus on the moment, but her thoughts kept drifting back to Talia. Her breath quickened. *What if something bad happened to her?* Carly's stomach churned as the minutes dragged on.

Stepping out of the bathroom, Carly held Taryn tightly against her chest, her eyes narrowing as she scanned the grim faces in the room. "I'm Carly Moore," she said, her voice barely above a whisper at first but growing stronger. "And this is our daughter, Taryn."

She placed Taryn back in the bassinet with care, her hands lingering for a moment on her daughter's soft blanket. She felt the stares from everyone in the room, but she refused to meet them. Her gaze stayed on Taryn, the one constant in this swirling storm of uncertainty.

"I can't tell you how difficult it is thinking that we're not safe here in your facility. I can say that Nurse Connie was very kind to me and our baby. We were recently given temporary custody of the baby that she took to the nursery. We would appreciate it if we were given the opportunity to sort this out privately as a family. I don't want the unpleasantries of sorting this out in public where I would have to share details of how you all thought *my* baby was abducted." She continued to look with warm eyes at her infant while avoiding the stares of everyone in the room. Then, she looked around the room. Focused with clear intent, she continued. "I'm sure my husband and his legal team, Attorneys Evan Moore and Ariel Dennison, along with Yara Shephard, his technical security specialist, would be glad to share the details of how the baby got to this floor and how we intend to leave with her in our custody." Evan stepped forward and handed the CEO his business card. Ariel opened her briefcase and handed the CEO the card with her legal practice information.

Evan spoke for the group. "We've been retained to represent the interests of the infant child, Talia Liliana Bradley."

The room fell into a tense, uneasy quiet as the hospital's team gathered in a loose huddle.

"We understand your position." The CEO faced Carly, his eyes wide.

Carly's heart pounded, her chest tight, as she waited, each second dragging out like an eternity.

"Do you want the baby now?" the hospital's chief counselor asked, breaking the silence.

"Yes," Carly said firmly, her voice cutting through the air like a blade. Her eyes locked onto the CEO's. "Now."

"I'll have the child brought to you." He turned to his team and summoned them out of the room before they left.

Finally, the door opened again. Nurse Connie entered, holding a small bundle swaddled in a blanket. Talia. Carly's breath caught in her throat as she reached out, her hands warmed with a mix of relief and fear.

"Come here, sweet girl. I'm here." Carly took Talia and placed her against the exposed skin on her chest just below her shoulder. Rubbing her back, Carly comforted the baby. "Talia Liliana." *Lily*. Carly looked at Nurse Connie, who appeared to be awaiting further instructions. "Thank you. That will be all."

Nurse Connie backed away and left along with security.

Yara looked at her best friend. "Now that's what I call a boss move. Hail to the empress."

Mace gave Carly an approving look and raised his hand in a toast. "Boss moves indeed."

But even with Talia safe in her arms, Carly couldn't shake the unease that still gnawed at her. Nothing felt certain. And that uncertainty haunted her, even in the calm of Talia in her arms.

CHAPTER TWENTY-NINE

CARLY gently placed the bassinets side by side, arranging the blankets so that the two tiny girls, Taryn and Talia, lay close enough to feel each other's warmth. She brushed her fingers over their soft cheeks, marveling at how they seemed to belong together, even in their innocence. Talia had just nursed for the first time, her small lips still slightly pursed as she settled into sleep. Carly felt a swell of emotions—love, protection, as the weight of their uncertain future pressing down on her chest.

Mace's voice, low and tender, broke through her thoughts. "Babe, I have so much to tell you."

He motioned for her to join him on the couch. The suite was quiet, just the sound of the babies' rhythmic breathing filling the air. Carly sank into the soft cushions, nestling into the crook of Mace's arm, drawing her legs up under her. The scent of him, warm and familiar, was a comfort she needed after the chaos of the past few days.

"Start at the beginning," she whispered, leaning her head on his shoulder, feeling the rise and fall of his chest as he exhaled deeply.

Mace's fingers traced lazy circles on her back, soothing her. "Simeon's going to spend the rest of his life in prison." His voice was steady but tinged with the weight of what had happened. "Yara… she had a big hand in the evidence against him."

Carly lifted her head, meeting his eyes. Sadness flittered in them, and she could see the toll the ordeal had taken on him. “How did she help?” she asked softly, her fingers resting against his chest, feeling the steady beat of his heart.

“She went to see Nala after everything went down,” Mace explained, his fingers twirling a lock of her hair. “Turns out, Simeon never contacted Nala, and Yara… she got her to confess. Simeon was trafficking drugs through the ports, and Nala knew about it. Worse than that, he gave the order to… get rid of you *and* her if it came to that.” His voice tightened, a barely controlled rage simmering beneath his calm exterior.

Carly’s body stiffened, the memories flooding back—the terror, the fear for her life and her baby’s. She closed her eyes, trying to push away the images of that night, but they clawed at her mind.

“I can’t go back to that day,” she whispered, her voice trembling. “It’s too much.”

Mace shifted, pulling her into his lap, holding her as if his embrace could shield her from the pain of the past. “You were incredible,” he murmured into her hair, pressing a soft kiss to the top of her head. “The doctors told me how strong you were, how you stayed conscious even when they drugged you. You saved yourself, Taryn, and… you saved me too.”

Carly looked up, searching his eyes, confusion clouding her gaze. “What do you mean, I saved you?”

Mace’s face softened, his hand cupping her cheek and his thumb brushing away the tear that had slipped down her face. “You’ve always been my heartbeat, Carly. I don’t know how I would’ve survived any of this without you. You make me appreciate life every day.”

She blinked away her own tears, her hand resting against his cheek as she smiled softly. “We’ve been saving each other for a long time, haven’t we?” Her voice wavered, but she felt the truth of her words in her bones. “I knew if I could just hold on until the sun came up, you’d find us. You always do.”

He kissed her, a soft, lingering kiss that spoke of years of shared dreams, struggles, and triumphs. But when he pulled away, there was something heavy in his eyes again. "It's been a tough stretch, but we're almost there. I hate to add more to our plate, but there's something you need to know. Emily Anne and her estranged husband… they were killed in a car accident last night."

Carly's breath caught, her fingers tightening around his. "Oh my God!" Her eyes darted to Talia sleeping peacefully in her bassinet. "What does that mean for her?"

Mace squeezed her hand. "Before Evan left, you told him you wanted to pursue custody of Talia if her mother didn't come back for her. Carly, I need to know… is that still what you want? Because if it is, we'll fight for her."

Carly's heart swelled as she looked at the two babies side by side. She had known the answer for a while now, though saying it aloud made it feel even more real.

"Yes," she said, her voice soft but sure. "I want to adopt her. She belongs to us, Mace. I felt it the moment I held her. We fought to bring her home from the hospital, but I need her to know she'll always have a family with us. I want her to feel safe. I want her to know she's loved."

Mace pulled her close, his forehead resting against hers. "Then we'll make it happen. I'll use every resource I have, every connection, to make sure she stays with us. You'll never have to do this alone, Carly. Whatever it takes, I'm right here."

She smiled through her tears, her heart filled with the certainty that no matter what came next, they would face it together. "Together," she whispered, the word a promise that no matter the obstacles, they were in this for the long haul.

Mace kissed her again, this time deeper, more urgent. His hands slipped into her hair as he pulled her closer, his lips moving against hers as though he was pouring everything he had into that moment. Carly melted into him, her body responding to the passion that surged between them, their love, their commitment, their unshakable bond.

When they finally pulled apart, breathless, Mace pressed his forehead to hers, his voice husky. “We’re building something beautiful here, Carly. Our family, our future… I promise you, we’ll figure it all out. Whatever it takes.”

Carly looked into his eyes, her heart full of love and hope. “We already have,” she whispered, and for the first time in a long time, she felt truly at peace.

Epilogue

Three years later.

Carly squinted against the blinding sun, lifting her hand to shield her eyes as she scanned the stadium filled to capacity. The roar of the crowd echoed around her, a blend of excitement and celebration, but all she felt was a deep sense of contentment. The wind teased at the oversized football jersey she wore, proudly displaying Mace's number twelve on the back. The fabric, loose and comfortable, pressed gently against her belly, revealing the soft curve beneath. Later this year, she and Mace would welcome their third child, completing the family they had always dreamed of.

At the center of the field, Mace stood tall among the officials preparing for the halftime ceremony. His jersey was about to be retired. He had told her once that the honor had been extended to him five years ago, but the timing hadn't felt right. And yet, even with the years that had passed, his records for most passes and yardage as a quarterback remained untouched. Now, as she watched him, pride swelled in her chest—this man, her husband, had always been her hero, not just on the field but in life.

Behind her, their tribe of well-wishers gathered: Mace's family, Aunt Nora, her brother John, Yara, and Ariel. Carly glanced at the girls, now three years old, standing close beside her. Taryn, just like her father, was the more outgoing of the two, her energy infectious even in this unfamiliar space. Carly smiled as she listened to the soft conversation between the sisters, their sweet voices rising above the crowd.

"What did it feel like being in Mommy's heart, Talia?" Taryn asked, her head tilted with curiosity. "She always says you're the baby of her heart."

Talia shrugged, her small shoulders lifting beneath her cheerleader uniform. "I don't know. You were in her heart and her belly, Taryn. What was that like?"

"I don't remember," Taryn replied, holding up her palms in an innocent gesture.

Both girls were dressed in matching cheerleader uniforms, complete with white sneakers and colorful ribbons in their hair. Talia, with her thoughtful expressions, often mirrored Carly's mannerisms, while Taryn had inherited her father's lopsided smile and warm, inviting eyes.

Taryn tugged on Talia's hand, her voice lowering into a whisper. "Do you think Daddy will save me from the bad man like he saved you?"

At that, Talia backed away slightly, moving to hide behind Carly's legs. Carly's heart clenched. The innocence in their voices was a stark reminder of the darkness they had overcome, and even though the girls didn't fully understand what had happened, their small minds had absorbed pieces of the past.

Mace, sensing Carly hadn't joined him on the field yet, turned around and waved for her to come forward. She smiled but shook her head, pointing at the girls. Without missing a beat, he jogged over, his strides sure and strong, cutting through the thrumming energy of the stadium.

He crouched down, scooping up Taryn first, then Talia, holding them securely in his arms. "What's going on, girls?" he asked softly, his voice tender as he addressed their worries.

"Will you save Taryn from the bad man?" Talia asked, her wide eyes searching her father's face. "We know you saved me from a bad man. We heard Mommy talking about it."

Carly's breath caught in her throat, her heart tightening with the weight of their words. She met Mace's eyes, a silent exchange of understanding passing between them.

Mace kissed both girls on their cheeks, his voice firm and gentle. "I will always protect you. No bad man, no matter what, will ever hurt my girls. Daddy loves you more than anything, and I'll always be here."

"Mommy too?" they asked in unison, their innocent faces turned up toward him.

"I'll always protect Mommy too," he promised, a smile breaking through the seriousness of his expression. He stood, still holding both girls, and turned to Carly. "Can you two do Daddy a favor?" His eyes softened as he spoke to his daughters. "Can you tell Mommy that it's time to go? Daddy needs Mommy by his side. I don't want to do this alone."

Taryn and Talia squirmed out of his arms and ran to Carly, tugging at her hand with urgency. "Come on, Mommy. Let's go!"

Carly laughed softly, her heart full as she let the girls lead her forward. With Mace walking proudly beside her, their family moved onto the field. The sun warmed her face, the same sun that had shone down on them years ago when she had stood in this very stadium, cheering for Mace as her favorite player. Now, ten years later, she walked beside him not just as his biggest fan, but as his wife, his partner, and the mother of his children.

This was their full-circle moment. As they stepped onto the field, Carly lifted her head, her heart swelling with the knowledge that everything they had gone through—the hardships, the love, the growth—had brought them to this place, right where they were always meant to be.

Acknowledgments

I would like to thank my husband, Tony, for your love and endless patience in completing this project. Special thanks to Mrs. B. L. Watson, Ms. D. Hunter, and Ms. J. Melvin for your support.

My thanks also go out to you, my dear readers. Thank you for reading and sharing my stories. I hope you all enjoy, Until the Sun Rises, a book in the second chance series.

ABOUT THE AUTHOR

Writing under the pen name of Michele Sims, a physician with years of professional experience and a storyteller, she pens stories frequently featuring multigenerational characters and delves into the complexities of love, family, and personal growth. Michele has received several accolades for her work, including as a 2024 finalist for the Diverse Readers' and Writers' Romance Book Award, the 2019 RSJ Debut Author Award, and the 2018 RSJ Aspiring Author Award. She lives in South Carolina with her husband, who has been her soulmate and greatest cheerleader. When not writing, she's engaged in exercise, travelling, listening to different genres of music, and observing the wonders of life on this marvelous planet. She has worked on several collaborative projects with other authors.

AUTHOR'S NOTE

Thank you for reading my book, Until the Sun Rises. If you enjoyed reading the book, please do us a favor and leave an honest review where you purchased it. I would also love to hear from you. Leave your comments for me at *michelesims2122@gmail.com*.

Sign up at authormichelesims.com with your email address for updates and giveaways.

Your support is appreciated.

My social media links:

FB Author Page: https://bit.ly/AuthorMicheleSimsFB
Newsletter: https://bit.ly/MSnewlet
Instagram: https://bit.ly/MSInstaNu
X: https://bit.ly/MicheleSimsX
BookBub: https://bit.ly/MSBookBub
Amazon: https://bit.ly/AmzMSimsU
Goodreads: https://bit.ly/MSGoodrds
Website: https://bit.ly/AuthorMSWebsite
Email: michelesims2122@gmail.com
Linktree: linktr.ee/MicheleSims
Pinterest: https://bit.ly/AuthorMSPins
Tiktok: https://bit.ly/AuthorMSTiktok
Youtube: https://bit.ly/AuthorMSYoutube
Threads: https://bit.ly/MicheleSimsThreads
Blue Sky: https://bit.ly/MicheleSimsBlueSky

www.ingramcontent.com/pod-product-compliance
Lightning Source LLC
LaVergne TN
LVHW091140080826
845145LV00008B/2210

* 9 7 8 1 7 3 4 7 5 6 7 9 1 *